Forever Classics

THE RIVER BETWEEN

Jacquelyn Cook

is an imprint of
Guideposts Associates, Inc.
Carmel, NY 10512

For Sandra
Who walked with me through history's pages

This Guideposts edition is published by special arrangement with Jacqueline Cook.

A Note From The Author
I love to hear from my readers! You may correspond with me by writing:

Jacquelyn Cook
1415 Lake Drive, S.E.
Grand Rapids, MI 49506

All Scripture quotations, unless otherwise noted, are taken from the King James version of the Bible.

Edited by Pamela M. Jewell
Designed by Kim Koning

Printed in the United States of America

CHAPTER 1

UHMMMMM! UHMMMMM!

The insistent drone of the steamboat's whistle floated up to Lily Edwards in the belvedere atop her father's home, interrupting her daydream. Somewhere, someone waited who could be one with her in mind and spirit as well as heart. She would not be rushed.

Uhmmmmm! The rousing blast drew her irresistibly to the rail. Looking across the treetops at billowing black smoke, she knew she must share in the excitement when the steamer docked. Mama would be angry if she went, but Mama wore a constant scowl these days because at eighteen, Lily was rapidly passing the age to make a suitable marriage. Wheet! Wheet! The short blasts of the whistle, punctuated with black puffs, told her that the paddlewheeler was nearing the wharf.

Lily tossed her long, dark curls, compressed her mushrooming skirt to fit the narrow staircase, and hurried down, singing out, "Emma, Emma, come quickly!" Her maiden aunt was the perfect chaperone for all occasions. Emma Edwards, still unmarried at twenty-five, was dependent for her livelihood upon the bounty of her sister-in-law's family. Young enough to sympathize with Lily's commitment not to marry simply to satisfy social custom, Emma sometimes wavered in her stand because she knew the heartbreak of being an old maid.

"Emma," Lily called again. She left the observatory and negotiated her voluminous crinoline through the attic and down another zigzag staircase to the second floor. She stood for a moment to catch her breath beneath the large, round grate in the hall ceiling. Barbour Hall was a magnificent white frame mansion built in the perfect symmetry of the Greek Revival. Since its construction in 1854, four years earlier, it was considered to be one of the finest examples of Italianate architecture in the South.

"What's the excitement?" Emma's calming voice answered as she emerged from the upstairs sitting room. Her features were set as usual in a placid expression that concealed her emotions as she waited to see what had evoked such enthusiasm.

"A steamboat's coming!" Lily exclaimed, "It's the signal for the *Wave*." Her brown eyes sparkling, Lily tugged at Emma's elbow. "Come with me. Hurry. We can't miss the landing!"

Emma hesitated but she so desired to be part of the crowd flocking to the riverfront. Nervously, she clutched her fists against her chest and twisted her fingers in the faded, gray muslin. "You know your mother expects me to make you behave like a lady."

"Oh, Emma, please," Lily's liquid brown eyes

became wistful. Her dainty face alight with curiosity about life, she bounced from one foot to the other while Emma considered.

Emma laughed. "You're as ebullient as a soap bubble and just as impossible to keep from floating away. We'll go—but you cannot be seen in that short-sleeved frock," she said in her measured, quiet way. "You must take time to put on a proper street toilet."

"Yes, of course, but do hurry." Lily's lilting voice came in excited bursts as she pulled her toward the spacious bedroom they shared. "At least my hair is already dressed." She looked at her reflection in the mirror over the marble-topped walnut dresser and fingered her dark brown hair that was pulled back from her face with tortoise shell combs into a cluster of long curls in back.

Whispering conspiratorily, they dressed quickly. From a tremendous walnut armoire in the back corner of the room, Lily chose a green silk dress with wide lace ruffles beginning at her shoulders, meeting in a point to emphasize her tiny waist, and spreading again to flow to her feet over the skirt held wide by her petticoat of stiff crinoline. She especially liked the sleeves with their lacy fullness at the wrists. The skirt Emma chose was elaborately trimmed with braid, and the frayed bodice she covered with a canezou, a dainty jacket fashioned with horizontal rows of smocking.

When they had donned tulle bonnets and gloves, they picked up tiny, silk parasols against the bright, June sun and tiptoed into the back bedroom where a closet concealed a hidden staircase. Silently, they slipped down the dark passageway, hoping they would not meet the servants.

Emerging in the back hallway, they hurried across the wide veranda that spread as gracefully around the house as the girls' billowing skirts. Indeed, Lily often fancied Barbour Hall looked like the belles of the day. The glassed belvedere formed her airy hat; the wooden balustrade, her neck ruffle; the green shutters on the upper story, her canezou; and the porch spreading around the first floor, her hooped skirt.

Lily had infected Emma with her sprightliness, and the girls bounced down the steep, brick steps and ran along the cleanly swept path through beds of fragrant summer flowers until they reached the stables.

The buggy ride took nearly half an hour as they proceeded down West Barbour Street trimmed by China trees. They descended the hill, passed the fine, brick storehouses and many churches of Eufaula, Alabama, and continued to the west bank of the Chattahoochee River.

From this high bluff they could look across the wide, dark blue water into the State of Georgia, which flaunted ownership of the river. Georgia had been one of the original thirteen colonies, but this side of the Chattahoochee had long remained territory occupied by the Creek Indian Nation.

Eufaula was a junction of stage lines with six-horse coaches going out into the frontier of Alabama. There were no railroads here, but the bluff, one hundred fifty feet above the low water mark, had become a steamboat landing even before the Creeks had been driven out. Because steamboats had plied the Chattahoochee since 1828, Eufaulians were cosmopolitan.

Turning the buggy to the left, the girls followed Riverside Drive past the Tavern, a two-story, English type with double galleries. Built in 1836, it was the first permanent structure in town. Thus far it had served as riverboat inn, private residence, and temporary church. The girls laughed about what it might become next as they rode on around the bend in the river and descended the hill to the wharf located at the foot of the bluff just north of the Tavern.

Reining the horse at a high vantage point they looked down as the tremendous, flat-bottomed boat, fully one hundred seventy-five feet long, belched fire and black smoke from her two towering smokestacks and glided to rest at the wharf. The huge, round paddlebox, which covered the machinery of her side wheel, was emblazoned with the name, *Wave*, and above that her insignia, a painting of a descending dove.

It was evident that Emma had forgotten her fear of Cordelia Edward's wrath. Quivering with excitement, she leaned forward to gaze at the upper deck where Lily was pointing.

"Would you look at that gown!" Lily exclaimed. "Um, my favorite green. It must be straight from Paris." She laughed as the lady fluttered her fan coquettishly and looked back at the young gentleman who strutted behind her like a peacock. Around them swirled bright colors of silks and satins as the fifty, first-class passengers milled about, chattering gaily, waving handkerchiefs, and promenading about the deck. They seemed to ignore the cacophony of piercing whistles, clanging bells, and shouting workmen.

Bales of cotton, piled everywhere along the wharf and on flat-bottomed barges, waited to be poled out for transfer to the steamer when the Italian marble, favored by Eufaula merchants and planters for the imposing mansions they were building in the Bluff City, was unloaded.

Emma motioned toward the police escort for the men carrying huge bags of silver, funds from the sale in Liverpool of the cotton crop that continued to grow larger each year.

Lily, however, was looking at the lower deck just above the water's edge where grizzled, unwashed passengers crowded amongst machinery, crates of merchandise, and all manner of freight. The steamboat mirrored southern society; there was no middle class. A woman whose hair was stringing about her wrinkled face pulled at four dirty children. Lily thought that her skirt drooped indecently around her limbs without the required number of petticoats.

Lily cocked her head to one side and pursed her lips in puzzled interest as a handsome young man, dressed in light, slim trousers and a dark, frock-tailed coat, moved into view behind the tired mother. Lily wondered why he was on the lower deck.

At that moment, a roustabout staggered backwards under the weight of a barrel and bumped into the especially well-dressed gentleman. His tall silk hat fell, revealing a head of neat, blond curls. As he whirled around, his chiseled features contorted with a rage his well-tended beard could not conceal.

Lily grimaced, glad that she could not distinguish his words for they were obviously a curse. Regaining his balance, the young man raised his gold-headed walking stick to deliver a blow. A slightly older man in a dark blue flannel uniform with a gold braid indicating that he was the captain, stepped quickly into the fray. He placed a restraining hand on the uplifted arm. Quietly, his face and manner pleasant, the ship's master reasoned with the hotheaded young man. The cowed roustabout retrieved the hat and the tall captain, obviously joking, clapped a hand on the petulant fellow's shoulder and guided him down the deck.

Admiring his calm self-assurance, Lily watched him intently as he went striding away. Seeming to feel her eyes upon him, he turned. Swiftly spanning the distance between them, his clear-eyed gaze met hers with a lively interest that made her blink and swallow as he stopped open-mouthed and held his breath mid-laugh. His smooth, tanned face warmed with a smile, lifting his dark mustache.

Sighing deeply, Lily tilted her head and lowered the silk fringe of her pink parasol. She smiled beneath it in spite of herself for she responded immediately to the look in his eyes. The pressure of Emma's hand on her arm reminded her wordlessly that this man was far beneath her social station. Knowing she would never again have a chance to meet anyone this exciting, she dropped her thick lashes and shielded her face with the parasol. "Let's go to Papa's office," she sighed.

Making their way through the jostling crowd past clean-smelling cypress lumber and the less pleasing aroma of salted fish, the girls entered the Cotton Exchange. In spite of the fact that Clare Edwards was surrounded by men all talking at once, he came forward to meet his daughter and sister with doting smiles and affectionate kisses.

Lily hugged her father lovingly. He was fifty-one, and when she thought of his growing so old, it made her sadly vow to keep his last days happy.

"I'm delighted to see my favorite beauties," he beamed, "but you should not be here."

"Oh, Papa, everyone in town is here."

"Yes, yes, but I mean you especially should not be here today," he hesitated. "It will seem forward."

Puzzled, Lily merely looked at her father who rubbed his hand over his balding head in confusion.

"There's something I should have told you," he faltered. "Come into my private office." He said nothing more until he was ensconced behind the enormous desk that Mama had bought for him. "You know how concerned your mother has been because you haven't. . . ." He cleared his throat and hesitated. ". . .haven't, uh, decided upon one of your beaux . . ."

"They are all just shallow boys!" Lily wailed. "I have lots of friends who are fun to be with at parties, but no one I want to spend the rest of my life with. I know Mama means well, but I wish she wouldn't push me so." She tried hard to swallow her anger. "I know Mama wants me to have the proper social position and security," she sighed disgustedly, "but I want more than that. I want a husband I can talk with, enjoy being with. Most of all he must share my faith in God!"

"I wouldn't trust my girl with less than a Christian gentleman," Papa replied. He cleared his throat again and his voice croaked, "But give this young man a chance."

"What young man?" Lily stirred uneasily, wondering how much longer she could struggle against Mama.

"Well, your mother wrote to her relatives in South Carolina. And if all has gone according to schedule, your distant cousin, Green Bethune, has journeyed aboard the river steamer *Wave*. You must leave quickly now before he comes in and thinks you are here to inspect him."

CHAPTER 2

THE CREAKING OF THE BUGGY made Lily grit her teeth. She clutched the red leather seat, and her stomach lurched with the jerking, swaying motion as she slapped the reins and headed the horse back up the hill toward Barbour Hall.

"You should be happy, Lily," Emma frowned anxiously. She pushed back golden tendrils of hair that were escaping the knot at the back of her head. "I'd be thrilled to be meeting an eligible new beau."

"I know," sighed Lily. Dread dulled her soft, dark eyes. Her delicate features puckered in a silent plea for understanding and help. "It looks as if Mama is waging an all-out campaign to get me married. It takes all the excitement out of courtship since she's placing a deadline."

"Try to keep an open mind," Emma begged, patting her hand, "and an open heart. Just keep telling yourself that you're about to meet someone special."

A rueful smile twisted Lily's flushed cheeks. "I'll

try." Never one to be pressed down for long, she straightened her shoulders and tossed her head so that the coils of her long curls bounced up and down like coffee-colored springs. Her spirits began to rise. "Meeting a man from a faraway place does sound exciting. I love to learn about new things," she said with her usual zest. "If I can just make Mama understand. . . ."

"Don't you sass her, now," Emma interrupted in alarm.

As they entered the rear of the wide central hallway, Lily's mother came puffing through the double doors at the entrance. Between them stretched a gracious receiving area made elegant by the fact that it contained only a few, carefully selected pieces of furniture. The narrow library table on which Mrs. Edwards now placed her gloves was fashioned in graceful curves entirely from one mahogany log. The two side chairs had been carved especially for this hall. The cool room was filled with the fragrance of roses. Two mass arrangements in matching, fan-shaped vases graced the marble shelves set below the murals on each side wall.

Seeing the girls before they could escape, Cordelia Edwards joined them at the back of the hall. She removed her bonnet wearily and said in a tone that indicated that it was she who must attend to everything, "I've been visiting Mrs. Treadwell who is dangerously ill." Sighing, she sank heavily to the hard sofa. Her attention was not upon them as she waited to catch her breath. With a small, self-satisfied smile, she smoothed her hand over the shiny, slick, black horsehair of her sofa with unusual "S" shaped legs. A particular treasure to her because this style was made only for a ten-year period around 1783. The sofa was smugly pointed out to visitors.

Standing on a square of the checkerboard black and white marble floor like a small pawn, Lily waited. "Lily!" Mrs. Edwards exclaimed. Her double chin shook as she noticed her daughter's outfit. "Why did you go out for a drive?" she snapped. "Why don't you ever do as you're told? I clearly said for you to take a nap this afternoon and look your best for a special dinner tonight." Without giving Lily a chance to reply she continued, "Go straight to your room and read First Samuel thirteen." She emphasized each syllable with a shake of her finger. "Think about what happened to Saul for being disobedient."

"Yes, ma'am."

Lily's hands trembled as she dressed for dinner in her favorite pink dotted swiss. Twirling before the looking glass, setting the tiered flounces of her skirt fluttering, she wondered if her cousin was as nervous as she was. Perhaps he did not know the reason for his invitation to visit. Her mother had not divulged a word to her, and she would think the dinner was special primarily because of the delicacies that had arrived from New Orleans aboard the steamboat if her Papa had not warned her.

Dear Papa. He tried to subscribe to the idea of a patriarchal family structure, but it was apparent to everyone that Mama was dominant. Even though his family was of the upper class with a social status equal to Mama's, she had brought far greater wealth into the marriage.

With a final pat to her hair, Lily started down the staircase. When she reached the landing she heard

Mama's artificial greeting voice and realized guests were arriving. From the large, oval landing, Lily could look down on the tops of their heads. Mama could not see her because between them hung the crystal teardrops of the "crown of thorns" chandelier. Just in case she might be noticed, Lily pretended to rearrange the flowers in the high niches, the coffin corners. She tried to catch snatches of conversation and prepare for her entrance. When the voice of a stranger rose above the others, she held her breath to listen.

"My dear Cousin Cordelia," the voice spoke in cultured tones, "may I present Captain Harrison Wingate?"

Startled at the words, Lily picked up her skirt daintily and moved to the head of the stairs just as the dark head, which was bent low over Cordelia Edwards's hand, lifted. Lily floated like a pink cloud down the grand staircase. The captain's tanned face brightened with delight and his dark mustache quivered as he drew in his breath and looked at her.

This time Lily met his gaze unashamedly. This was a man who faced life head on. Smiling demurely with her head cocked to one side, she waited back a pace. She could tell that her mother was struggling for self-control while the blond, curly-haired younger man continued speaking.

"Captain Wingate and I have become such fast friends during the trip from Apalachicola Bay that I was certain you'd want me to extend your hospitality," he said suavely.

He turned his head slightly, and Lily recognized his golden beard as the one she had seen on the deck of the steamboat. As she moved nearer, he swung around. His eyes lazily assessing her from head to toe told her that he did indeed know of her existence and of the reason for his visit. With her guard stiffened, she watched in amusement as Mama wavered between indignation that he had brought a common steamboat captain to her dinner party and the desire to establish a good relationship with a possible future son-in-law.

"Yes, of course," Mrs. Edwards murmured. Glancing up at Lily in relief, she continued with more assurance, "May I present my daughter, Lily, Captain Wingate, and this, dear, is your cousin Green Bethune. Of course you've heard me speak of my darling second-cousin-once-removed, Lizzie Bethune, of the South Carolina Bethunes," she gushed. "This is her youngest son who has just arrived for a lovely visit with us."

Both gentlemen kissed Lily's extended hand and she murmured polite greetings to them equally; however, other guests began arriving and Cordelia Edwards drew her handsome cousin back to the doorway.

"Green, dear, come meet one of our most illustrious citizens, Edward B. Young, who built our first bridge across the Chattahoochee, started the Union Female College, established a bank and sawmill and store and, oh, so many things—Mr. and Mrs. Young, this is my cousin, Green Bethune of the Carolina Bethunes."

"Welcome to Alabama, young man," the distinguished gentleman said cordially. He launched into a discussion of business.

Freed from having to converse with Green Bethune until she could prepare herself, Lily looked across the expanse of the entrance hall trying to catch Papa's eye. Standing by the double entrance doors, which were framed by beautifully etched side lights, he was engrossed in conversation with the Reverend and Mrs. Steele and did not notice her. Lily stepped up to greet some of her favorites, Maximilian Wellborn and his wife. The Shorters and the Kendalls were arriving, but she suddenly realized that Captain Wingate was standing back by the stairs—alone.

Embarrassed by her mother's rudeness in not introducing him to anyone, Lily moved quickly to his side and graciously invited him into the parlor. She guided him across the spacious room where they could stand in some seclusion by the white, Italian marble fireplace. She had spoken to him to be kind, thinking to put him at ease in an odd situation. It was she, however, who fidgeted nervously. The tall man, in his dark dress clothes stood casually in command.

She cleared her throat. "Um. You must lead an exciting life, Captain, so fraught with danger—the peril of death at every turning. . ."

She smiled up at him. Her cheeks, radiating the glow from the myriad of candles in the Waterford chandelier, relaxed from the tension of matchmaking as her eyes rested on his calm face.

Harrison Wingate chuckled and answered quietly, "Oui, it's exciting, and yes, I enjoy the challenge of what may lie around the bend, but the danger. . . ." He shrugged it off with a wave of his hand. "It's not so great if you know the inner depths and precisely where the Chattahoochee conceals her perils." He chuckled again. "Why, just the other day a man fell overboard. I was up top on the hurricane deck when I looked down and saw him floundering. 'I can't swim,' he shrieked. 'Help, help, I'll drown!' " Captain Wingate's eyes twinkled. "I yelled down to him, 'Can you stand?' He gasped that he could. 'Then stand up, man,' I commanded him. He stretched out his legs—we were over a sandbar," he laughed. "He was in two feet of water."

Lily giggled and clapped her hands in delight. The distinctive way he pronounced certain words with an ever so slight curl of his lip around a syllable kept her intrigued. He seemed quite nice, not at all the rake she had been led to believe river people to be. "You must be proud of the *Wave*," she said.

"Yes, she's a beautiful vessel," he nodded. "Didn't I see you when we landed?"

"Shhh, don't let Mama hear you," she pressed her finger to her lips, giggled, and inclined her head closer. "We weren't supposed to go, but I just couldn't miss it."

Harrison Wingate's eyes twinkled and he smoothed his mustache that quivered over an amused smile. "Where is your sister? I haven't seen her."

"My sister, oh, Emma. She's my aunt and chaperone. Mama probably has her supervising the dinner." She ran her finger over one of the Sévres vases on the gold leaf shelving around the huge Belgian mirror that reflected them and studied him surreptitiously. His grammar evinced good breeding and, although his hands had a strength that showed he had worked, he had the clean fingernails of a gentleman.

Lily and the captain were suddenly bathed in warmth as the last rays of the sun flooded through the lace draperies. A rosy glow washed over the ivory-white walls and even the ceiling mouldings, painted shades of pastel lavender and edged in gold leaf, gleamed. Every window in the house reached from the floor to within a few feet of the eighteen-foot ceilings. Happily, Mama had made only valances in heavy wine velvet. Lily reveled in sunlight.

Relaxed, she wanted to know more about Captain Wingate's travels on the river that gave their kingdom of cotton access to the world. The thousands of bales being shipped down the Chattahoochee to Apalachicola, Florida, not only made it the largest cotton-exporting port in America but also gave exceptional prosperity to Eufaula.

"It must give you a tremendous feeling of power to transport the product on which the lives of everyone in this area depend."

"Well," he laughed self-deprecatingly, "about the time I start feeling like God's overseer on the river, some planter's wife sends me shopping. Right now in my stateroom lies a new gown especially prepared by a shop on Royal Street in New Orleans. The lady gave me orders to use all my energy to save her gown if the boilers explode and the steamer sinks."

Lily was surprised at the pang of jealousy this gave her. "I wish I could travel," she said wistfully. "I'd enjoy meeting interesting new people."

"Many are traveling," he said eagerly. "Europeans are touring our country—and hordes of people are moving West."

"Yes," she agreed. "A number from the Southern Rights group here moved to 'bleeding Kansas' in order. . . ." She winced, remembering her mother's repeated warnings that men did not like a woman who was too intelligent. "In order to vote," she finished lamely.

Harrison Wingate apparently did not know that a lady should not talk about politics. He began a lively discussion of the widening gap between North and South.

Exhilarated by the interesting conversation, Lily was surprised by a touch at her elbow.

"Cousin Lily, I'm to escort you to dinner, I believe," Green Bethune said suavely, bowing and offering his arm. "That's a mighty pretty frock you're wearing this evening," he drawled.

She nodded toward the Captain, turned and grasped the proffered arm with stiff fingers. She felt painfully aware that it was intended for her to marry this man, but as they passed into the music room where the square grand piano of carved rosewood was being played, her tension eased and her pink slippers kept time to the lively plinking. Green patted her hand on his elbow and looked at her as if she were the most beautiful creature he had ever met. Lily could see by their reflection in the towering pier mirror behind the piano that they did make a handsome couple. Green bowed gallantly as she proceeded him through the sliding doors into the dining room.

Responding flirtatiously to his charm, Lily inclined her head, and dimpled her most coquettish smile. "Thank you, kind sir."

The dining room was a place of glittering beauty. Flames from dozens of candles twinkled in the prisms of the chandeliers that hung low over each end of the mahogany table. Their light glimmered in the mirror plateau on the mahogany sideboard.

Lily was glad that the butler had swiftly added a place for Captain Wingate and Emma had hurriedly changed her frock and joined the group as his dinner partner. They brought the number seated at the long, elegantly set table to twenty-four.

As the first course, spicy turtle soup, was being served, Green Bethune smiled ingratiatingly at Lily and said, "Tell me about Eufaula. I thought I was coming to the western frontier to meet a girl in buckskin or calico at the very least, and here you are a belle in the latest Paris gown."

Lily's laughter filled the air. "Our urbanity is a surprise, I suppose. Being a riverport makes the difference. Alabama has been a frontier in constant struggle between Spanish, French, English—and of course, Indians. This county, Barbour, is in a territory that was one of the last strongholds of the Creek Indian Nation."

"But you achieved statehood as early as 1819, did you not?" he asked as red snapper courtbouillon on mounds of rice was served.

"That's right," she replied, noticing his polished table manners. "But the Creeks remained. Whites began intruding on them and there was a war in 1827—"

"—When Carolina was nearly two hundred years old," Green said with a slightly superior sniff.

Lily nodded assent. "The Indians signed a treaty in 1832, ceding their lands east of the Mississippi, but many remained here. . . ." She faltered as she saw Mama glaring at her from the end of the table. Proud of her good brain, Lily thrust out her lower lip and continued doggedly. "One of the tribes was the Eufaulas which gave the town its original name." Lily paused to take a helping of butter beans. Green nodded laconically, but his attention was on the fish.

"The first white settlement here, called Irwinton, was established around 1835, with men like Lore, Wellborn, Irwin, Iverson, Moore, and Robertson developing the town." Lily could feel the warmth of eyes upon her face. Down the table, Captain Wingate was leaning forward to see and hear her. Quickly dropping her eyes to her plate, she sampled the succulent snapper before finishing.

"Cotton was already being shipped from here," she hesitated, speaking stiffly now, oddly flustered by the captain's gaze. "Even though there was still fighting with the Indians for another year. By 1842, this was a thriving town. Ironically, it was free of Indians by then, but they decided to go back to the Indian name," she laughed self-consciously.

"My, you are an eager young woman," Green replied lazily, turning toward the cinnamon fragrance wafting from the sweet potato soufflé. "I didn't expect a complete history lesson from such a pretty head," he added in a deliberate drawl.

Lily could feel her cheeks turning red. "Our early days have been colorful—but I'm afraid I've bored you with too many facts," she finished lamely.

"Oh, no, not at all." Green's deportment was exquisitely correct, but the glazed expression in his eyes showed no interest in the struggles of the early settlers.

Dessert arrived—rich chocolate molds with butter cream filling and praline topping—and then the ladies were excused. Papa passed cigars and the eminent jurist, John Gill Shorter, launched a political discussion about the Dred Scott Decision. His impassioned words were cut off as the gentlemen moved across the hall to the library. Lily wanted to hear more about the Supreme Court case that had brought the ongoing debate about slave states and free territory to a head and inflamed and divided the nation; but, of course, ladies were excluded from such talk.

"Emma," Lily said softly, linking arms with her confidante as they drifted into the wide receiving hall. "I'm so glad you got to join the party, but Mama was furious because Green invited the Captain."

"Well, you made your usual conquest," Emma whispered. "All he could talk about over dinner was your delicate beauty, your superior intelligence, your thoughtfulness. . . ."

"No! Really?" Lily's dark eyes sparkled. "I genuinely liked him, too. Why must all of the men Mama considers suitable husbands be so insipid?"

"Didn't you like Green?"

"Oh, he's handsome and charming, but—well, I don't know. He asked me a question and didn't even listen to the answer." Lily felt Mama glaring at her again. The ladies had been seated in the music room where a string quartet had begun a Bach Fugue. The girls took seats on the carved side chairs in the hall and politely sipped their demitasse.

When the gentlemen rejoined them, most of them were discussing the cotton crop, but Lily caught Green's hushed, excited voice telling the captain about a friend in New Orleans who had challenged one of the local colonels because of a slight insult and had been shot to death in a duel.

Soon, all of the guests were bidding them a good-night; when the last ones had departed, Lily climbed slowly, thoughtfully, up the stairs to her bedroom at the front of the house. Putting on her light muslin nightgown, she tried to sort out her feelings. This had been such a stimulating day that she sat for a long while before her roll-top lady's secretary trying to collect the thoughts she wished to record. Gazing unseeingly into the mirror over the small desk, she had just lifted her journal from one of the side bookshelves when the door to her room burst open.

"Lily, my dear child," Mama paused to puff, "I hope you are ready to become a bride."

CHAPTER 3

"OH MAMA!" LILY WAILED. "If you mean Green, we've barely met!" Her face pinched with distress. "Please don't make me decide so soon."

Cordelia Edwards sat heavily on a small, cherry rocker. "Oh, pshaw, you know I don't mean you'd be married tomorrow. I want to keep my baby a little while longer, too. But, darling, we must plan for your future. What would our friends think if you weren't married before your nineteenth birthday?" She sighed heavily and began loosening her clothing that stretched tightly over her girth.

"But, Mama, it's not that I feel too young to get married," Lily said hurriedly because her mother was obviously about to retire for the night. "I want someone special, somebody who—"

"Green is all you could desire. He's a handsome man!"

"Yes, but. . ."

"He's from one of the first families of South

Carolina. He has ample wealth to keep you in Paris gowns."

"There's more to life than Paris gowns." Lily's lower lip thrust out, and she drew shaky breaths as she fought tears.

Mrs. Edwards jerked in surprise. The cherry rocker creaked. "I really must speak to Mr. Edwards about your insolence."

"I'm sorry," she sighed, "I—I didn't mean to be rude, but you don't understand my feelings." Lily clenched fistfuls of her muslin gown and looked beseechingly at this woman who lived on such a different emotional plane. Her whole world revolved around social functions and friendly gossip. Lily knew she was a fine, Christian woman who constantly did works of charity for the sick and the poor, but she somehow remained above them, untouched with love.

"No, I don't understand you," she was saying. "I'm merely telling you to enjoy the courtship of a *beau ideal*. You can have a long period of engagement." She moved wearily to the door, then turned back. "However, be prepared within the month to set a wedding date."

For a long while after her mother had left the room, Lily stood by one of the wide, square windows and looked out at the stars. The realization that her mother would never understand the intensity of her convictions turned the happiness of her day to melancholy. All the while Mama pushed her into marriage and adulthood, she treated her like a child, making little difference between her and her adolescent brother, Foy. Somehow she was afraid that she and her mother would never share the same view of life or the joy of being two adults together.

Sighing, she turned to the soft comfort of her bed. Delicate rosewood posts, rising high above her head, supported a graceful, curved frame and an airy, macramé canopy. The snowy counterpane required a close look to distinguish the white on white design of leaves outlined with dainty knots of candlewicking. Satin-stitched grapes added another texture. She always felt secure in its soft comfort. Kneeling on the stool beside the high bed, she folded her hands in prayer.

"Dear heavenly Father, I know that your Word tells me to honor my parents and obey them, but please help me now. I know thou didst create marriage as an extension of Thy love. Guide me to the one who will share my faith in Thee, who will love me better because he first loves Thee. Help me to follow Thy will that I may give my life in service to Thee. In Jesus' name, I pray. Amen."

Climbing into the feather bed, she pretended to be asleep when Emma came into the room, but she knew that the tears slipping down her cheeks would give her away.

Sunlight, streaming through the huge windows and dancing from the bright blue walls to the deep blue and white Oriental rug, awakened Lily in a happy frame of mind. She was glad that her room was on the east side of the house for she loved the early morning. She went into her dressing room to wash her face in the Wedgwood lavatory set in a marble slab. As she grasped the small, porcelain handles of the German silver faucets to cut on the running water, she had to admit that wealth was nice. Papa's own waterworks were a part of the original construction of this house. Water was pumped by a windmill to a cistern in the attic and the drop from the attic gave pressure.

She breakfasted from an enameled tray brought up the hidden stairs by one of the maids. Hot biscuits, honey, and tea were served on her favorite tea set. The white ridges of the china were studded with pink roses and someone had added a fresh rose to the tray. Brushing out the tight coils of her hair, she let it float loosely around her shoulders and she tied a white ribbon in a flat bow on top of her head. After she had dressed in cool, white organdy, she glanced out of the window and saw a dark-suited man rounding the red cedars at the front gate.

"Captain Wingate!" she whispered to herself in surprise. He was no doubt calling to leave his card in the tray on the library table in the entrance hall to express his appreciation for their hospitality. Knowing Mama might be obviously condescending to him, Lily flew down the stairs as swiftly as was decorously possible.

"Good morning, Captain Wingate," she smiled warmly, meeting him on the veranda with her hand extended. The flounces of her skirt billowed frothily around her.

"Miss Lily! What a delightful pleasure." He bent low, taking her small, white hand in his strong, tanned fingers. "I wanted to thank your mother for her hospitality."

"Yes, well," Lily glanced surreptitiously over her shoulder, hoping Mama was not up. "Perhaps she's sleeping late. I'll convey your appreciation. Uh, would you like to see the garden?"

"I'd enjoy that very much."

They started around a walk that had been swept with a brush broom early that morning. Everything was fresh with the lush greenness of early June. They strolled in silence past neatly edged flower beds spilling over with a colorful mixture of perennials.

Dwarfed beside a spreading clump of palms, Lily paused and pointed to the huge fans. "This windmill palm was brought a few years ago from Berckmann's Nursery in Augusta, Georgia," she said stiffly, her mind on what Mama would say if she caught her promenading with the steamboat captain. "You'll see several of them around town; they are becoming quite a tradition for Eufaula."

"Nice, but that planting of oak-leaved hydrangeas is more to my liking," he said as they moved on by a pine-shaded bed on the west side of the house. A soft breeze rustled the pine needles on the trees high above their heads and wafted the fragrance of the drooping hydrangea blossoms around them.

"Yes," she agreed. "I really like native plants in naturalized settings, too." She smiled up into his warm eyes that were alive with interest in both her and the surroundings. She was beginning to feel comfortable with him and to forget about Mama. He did not seem to possess any of the less savory characteristics usually associated with the itinerant river population who were said to frequent the taverns and gambling houses.

Not wanting Mama to look down from her bedroom window and see them, Lily led him to the kitchen herb and vegetable garden. Beginning to chat casually, they walked between raised beds of tansy, beebalm, chives, parsley, dill, rosemary, and sweet marjoram. Captain Wingate's foot crushed sun-warmed leaves of mint that had escaped into the path and released a clean, mouth-watering fragrance.

"Peach?" Lily asked, suddenly hungry as they passed a small tree bending low with rosy fruit.

"*Merci,*" he smiled.

Peeling back the fuzzy skin, they bit into the soft yellow flesh. Tangy juice trickled down their chins. Laughing, they rounded a clump of pampas grass, which furnished plumes for parlor decorations during the winter, and crossed under the walkway that connected the house with the brick kitchen. Opening a wrought iron gate, Lily led the way back into the formal garden of boxwood-edged beds.

"Stop!" Harrison grasped her hand with peach-sticky fingers.

Catching her breath at his touch and the soap-scented nearness of him, she turned her eyes from his face toward his pointing finger with difficulty.

Silently they watched a tiny hummingbird. Its round, green body and blur of wings made an enchanting picture as it darted from one deep-throated orange lily to another. Barely drawing breath, they said nothing until the exquisite creature had flown to the top of a tall pine. Each seemed to feel the other a kindred spirit. She had not realized they were still clasping hands until a hardy voice broke their shared silence.

"Good morning you two."

Self-consciously, they drew apart physically, and turned to see Green Bethune striding toward them from the direction of the guest quarters that were reached from the back porch with an entrance entirely separate from the rest of the house.

"Good morning, Cousin Lily." He inclined his head in a slight bow. "How are you, old chap?" He clapped Harrison on the shoulder and continued exuberantly, "How about riding back to town with you? I have business with John McNab at his bank."

"Actually, I walked up," replied Harrison quietly.

"All that way?"

"I'm sure Papa would be delighted for you to use the stables," Lily said.

"Why don't you come with me and combine business with pleasure?" Green smiled down at her. "Perhaps you could shop while I set up my banking and make some appointments."

"Well, perhaps," she hesitated. "I didn't realize you had business here."

"Why, of course," he laughed. "I'm a cotton broker for my father's firm. I'm here to buy cotton for shipment directly to Liverpool." He paused, smirked, and added in a deliberate drawl, "This trip was not entirely pleasures." His glazed blue eyes moved over her in a knowing way that reddened Lily's cheeks. "Come along and show me the town."

"All right," Lily agreed. "Why don't y'all wait in the summerhouse while I collect my hat and shawl and Emma to accompany us," she smiled and gestured toward the wicker chairs in a white-latticed, octagon-shaped enclosure festooned with lacy green leaves of wisteria vines.

Lily was always glad to include Emma as her chaperone. Her sweet disposition and calm temperament smoothed any occasion, and her primary pleasure in life came through sharing Lily's happy times.

When the girls returned to the gazebo, Lily's twelve-year-old brother, Foy, was excitedly hopping from one foot to the other as Captain Wingate told him about the cages of circus lions and bears he had recently transported.

As the laughing group headed the carriage down Barbour Street, Lily pointed out the place next door where the distinguished gentleman, Colonel Lewis Llewellen Cato was building a Greek Revival mansion.

"He's a member of the Eufaula Regency, the Southern Rights group I was telling you about," she said, turning to nod at Captain Wingate in the back seat with Emma. "He's a leader in the secessionist movement."

She started to point out to Green how the four important thoroughfares, Livingston, Orange, Randolph and Eufaula were laid out to spell L-O-R-E in honor of the early leader Seth Lore; however, seeing that her cousin actually cared nothing for learning about the town and its people, she settled back against the red leather seat of the fringe-topped carriage and let Green entertain them with tales of his escapades back home in Charleston.

They left Green at the iron-grille-work entrance to the Eastern Bank of Alabama. Wingate strolled with the ladies. They wandered through the apothecary shop and various dry goods merchants. At the confectioner's, he bought rock candy.

As they stood crunching the candy, Lily noticed that Green rejoined them from the opposite direction of the bank.

"My business is finished for the morning," he declared. "How about a horseback ride? We've grown soft in that floating hotel of yours, Harrison, old man." He clapped the tall man on the shoulder.

Lily thought that Green, not Harrison, looked soft, but she readily agreed to the exercise because she enjoyed fresh air and sunshine.

Emma was not an enthusiastic horseback rider like Lily. As they changed to riding habits, Lily could tell by the grim expression on Emma's pale face that sometimes being her chaperone was a chore. Lily loved her devotedly and wished Mama did not treat her so nearly like a servant. In their realm of society, there was no acceptable work for a husbandless lady. The only choice was to live on the charity of the nearest relative, reaping few rewards while devoting total energy to another woman's family. Smiling at her as they went back downstairs, Lily was glad that Emma could get out and have some fun with her instead of staying in the back room at the spinning wheel. So many unmarried girls had there earned the name spinster.

While Emma was being helped to mount the gentle mule she preferred, Lily placed her foot in the stirrup and sprang into her sidesaddle unassisted. From the moment her shining black horse felt her weight, he sprang into a lope, lifting front feet, back feet, and speeding away with a long, easy gait. Laughing, her dark hair streaming behind her. Lily knew that the men were surprised. Their horses would probably not reach a lope without first breaking into a trot.

Exhilarated, Lily led the way down the red clay road cut deeply between high banks. Whipping his horse, Green gave chase through the pine-scented woodland. They clattered past a strange-looking field where a spring tornado had snapped off pine saplings waist high. Reining in, laughing, they waited for the others to catch up.

"This field reminds me of one back home," Green said as they walked the horses in pace with Emma's mule. "My brother and I had a yoke made to fit yearling calves. We'd yoke a pair and put small boys from the quarters on their backs. Then we'd run 'em through the stumps. The boys could hang on pretty well because the yearlings could swing their back feet in opposite directions so we tied the tails together."

The girls looked at him, uncomprehending. Visualizing the scene, Harrison nodded.

Green explained, "They'd start to run, and wham, the yoke would hit a stump. It was great sport to watch who could hold on and who would go sailing over the calf's head." He laughed heartily, slapping his thigh.

"How mean!" declared Emma, her face pink with indignation and too much sun.

"You should've been whipped," laughed Lily.

They dismounted at a fern-banked creek and drank deeply at a spring bubbling out clear and cold. As they rested in the shade, Lily prevailed upon the Captain to tell them more of his colorful river travel. While he talked quietly, she sat smiling happily. Emma relaxed with her hands in her lap and listened attentively. Her blue eyes showed enjoyment instead of being shuttered against the world as they usually were. The morning passed quickly. Laughing, they foraged along the roadside, plucking a few late plums from the scrubby bushes. The tart, yellow fruit merely whetted their appetites. Clucking to the horses, they galloped back toward Barbour Hall.

When they reached the stables, a servant met them saying that Green had a message. Flinging his reins toward a stableboy, he hurried to the house. Slowly, tiredly, Emma followed.

Holding back with a show of making certain Prince was being properly rubbed down, Lily tenderly stroked the black velvet between his nostrils. Flattening her other hand beneath Prince's huge lips, she let him nip sugar from her palm.

Harrison Wingate stood watching, smiling.

"Um, Captain, won't you stay and dine with us," she said hesitantly, praying Mama wouldn't explode.

"Thank you," he said quietly "but I—I've been away from my duties far too long now. I must go." He remained unmoving. Searching her face, he leaned toward her and reached out to pat the horse's nose. "Beautiful animal," he said softly.

Lily held her breath as his eyes locked hers.

"May I see you again?"

"Oh, I want to, but Mama—I'm afraid she wouldn't allow. . ." She looked into his tanned face, so gentle yet so strong and said softly, "I'll be going to prayer meeting tonight, but I don't suppose that you. . ."

Harrison laughed good-humoredly. "You don't imagine sailors to be religious? God speaks to me in nature—here in your beautiful garden and in the stars when I'm alone at night on the river." His hand was nearly touching hers on the velvet nose. "With the danger from the snags along the river, one must have faith in God's personal care, but I miss the opportunity for the fellowship and strengthening which come from attending church."

Emma was returning to see what had detained her. Quickly, Lily whispered the address of the church.

When she entered the house without Harrison Wingate, Green had attended to his business, and the family assembled in the dining room. Lily's appetite leaped when she saw the huge soup tureen on its stand on the sideboard because that meant gumbo. When the top was lifted, she breathed deeply of the pungent aroma. Their cook, Dilsey, had a magical way of mixing herbs in a well-guarded secret recipe. She always beamed and winked at Lily when she turned party leftovers into Lily's favorite dish. Ravenously, Lily ladled a lavish amount of the thick gumbo over the mound of steaming rice in her flat soup bowl.

Cordelia Edwards gushed over their young guest. "You have charmed everyone, Green, dear. Invitations are pouring in. You two young people are going to a house party next week at Roseland Plantation," she beamed.

"Come with me this afternoon," said Papa. "There's enough cotton stored in the warehouses here to fill all your ships bound for Liverpool and keep those new power looms in Lancashire whirring for a long time." Papa's voice croaked, "Then you'll be free to enjoy yourself."

After the meal, Lily intended to slip to her room by way of the hidden staircase. She had just reached the back hall when she was stopped by a hand on her arm.

"Lily," Green whispered, "I thought I'd never catch you alone."

Lily whirled just as he had anticipated and found herself encircled in his arms. His bristly beard rubbed her face as he tried to kiss her. She pushed away. "Mr. Bethune! Behave yourself! I'm surprised at you trying to take such liberties. The servants will see." She wrenched back from his grasp in his momentary hesitation and stepped out on the back porch because she knew it would be used by the servants on their way across the high, covered walkway to the brick kitchen.

"You were quick enough to hold hands with Harrison in the garden this morning—oh, I saw you."

"You—you misunderstood. He took my hand to show me something."

"What?"

"It was a humming—oh, you wouldn't understand." She shook her head, and her hair bounced around her shoulders. "I was trying to be nice to your friend, to keep Mama from insulting him."

Green smiled and reached out to squeeze a bouncing, brown curl. "You're sure you weren't trying to make me jealous?"

"Of course not! You know my parents would never allow me to have a suitor. . ." she swallowed, "below my station."

"You really don't know that the Wingates could buy. . ."

Kitty, one of the servants, came along the covered passageway carrying the silver tureen. Green dropped his hand, straightened back away from her, and said nothing more until the tall girl had moved past with her ebony face averted. He resumed the conversation reflectively. "No, I'm sure your parents are careful about your suitors. I guess that's why you sent for me."

"I certainly did not send for you!" Lily snapped, exasperated. "I knew nothing at all about it until after you'd arrived." Her cheeks were flaming.

"Harrison said you were watching the dock. I assumed you were eager to get married. As lovely as you are, we will have beautiful children."

Lily stamped her foot and tears of embarrassment filled her eyes. "I was merely out for a lark. I had no idea you existed. Furthermore, I'm in no hurry to get married," she retorted angrily. "It's all Ma–ma." Her voice became a wail and tears spilled over in spite of all she could do.

"I'm sorry," Green said with genuine contrition. "I

really did misunderstand. I'm in no hurry to get married either. Let's just have fun and see what develops."

She nodded, sniffling, and left him to go to her room. Relieved that Papa had requested the young man to accompany him to the Cotton Exchange for the afternoon, she was happier still that he declined her invitation to attend prayer meeting that evening, although, she doubted that he would have chosen to ignore her had he suspected that she might encounter Harrison Wingate.

When Lily and Emma arrived at the white-frame church, Harrison already stood on the steps by the gentlemen's door. Of all times, Foy had chosen to accompany them. At least she was thankful that Mama and Papa had pleaded weariness and gone to bed early; however, she wondered if Foy had been spying and had suspected that Wingate would be there. She knew that the most glamorous occupation imaginable to a barefoot, southeast Alabama boy was steamboat captain or river pilot.

His chubby cheeks glowing, Foy rushed worshipfully to Harrison's side and kept them from having a private greeting. Emma glanced at her like a frightened bird and clutched her fists against her chest, but she said nothing as they entered and took their seats on the ladies' aisle.

Reverend Steele spoke eloquently from the Book of Acts about Peter's vision while praying on the rooftop. Lily had nearly memorized the story that told of the animals being let down in a sheet and Peter protesting that he had never eaten anything common or unclean; consequently, her mind strayed to the

Captain. All too often her eyes lifted from the Bible to look across the church to the men's side at his strong profile that indicated so much character.

After the service she whispered to Emma, "Please stay for choir practice without me. I'll be in the churchyard."

Emma chewed her lips. Doubt played over her features that were made plainer by the fact that her pale hair was parted in the middle and pulled back severely into a knot at the back of her neck.

"Please, Emma!" She squeezed the older girl's arm. "Please."

Emma turned aside wordlessly, and Lily sighed thankfully when she saw Foy darting about with a group of boys in the lengthening shadows of dusk.

"I was praying I'd get to speak with you alone." Harrison stirred in the semi-darkness beneath a giant oak.

Lily laughed uncertainly. "I'm afraid I was, too," she whispered as she joined him.

"The *Wave* leaves at dawn."

"Oh."

Emboldened by the small, hurt sound she made, Harrison hurried on. "We're only going to Columbus," he said, referring to the Georgia town that was eighty-five miles up the Chattahoochee at the head of navigation. "We'll reach there tomorrow afternoon and be loaded for return to Apalachicola. I had hoped to stay in Eufaula for a short while, but the boiler on the sidewheeler *Emily* exploded. She was loaded with cargo and furniture, and she burned to the water's edge. We'll have to take the next load that was intended for her."

Lily winced. "Yes, I heard that seven lives were

lost. Do be careful. I've heard the Chattahoochee called the longest graveyard in the State of Georgia."

"Don't you worry," he smiled at her tenderly. "I have a good pilot, and I'm trying to put in extra safety precautions and keep the crew watching for logs and snags and sand bars."

"I know it must be an exciting life." She looked up at him with eyes full of admiration. "I always enjoy it when Mama decides we can take a trip."

"The *Wave* has excellent staterooms," Harrison replied eagerly, "and the ladies saloon is. . ." He stopped and searched her face as if memorizing it. "I'll be back by here in a few days. I have to take a big load of cotton down river for Green. It will be transferred to his deep-draft sailing ships and go directly to Liverpool. May I call upon you before I leave for the Florida coast?"

Lily's mind blocked out all of the many reasons she should say no. It pulsated with only one word. "Yes," she breathed.

The church doors opened and the chattering choir spilled across the yard. Swiftly, before Lily was swept away, Wingate bent over her hand, pressed a kiss upon it, and whispered, "*Au revoir*."

Floating, she did not remember returning home. Surprised that she was in her room, she dreamily removed petticoat after petticoat, hoops, slippers, and prepared for bed. She opened her roll-top desk, but she was unable to settle down to her journal or to sleep. She climbed through the darkness of the attic and then took the two more short flights to the belvedere. Lily's delight was that Papa had crowned the house with this observatory that was larger than an ordinary cupola. With its three floor-to-ceiling windows on the front and back and two on each side, she felt at one with the sky. When she reached the top, she was disappointed to find Foy there before her.

"Well, Sister!" Foy looked up from the table where he had spread his astronomy books. His round cheeks dimpled a grin and his dark eyes snapped devilishly in the light of his hurricane lantern. "What'll you give me not to tell that you met the Captain?"

"There's nothing to tell," she tossed her dark hair and thrust her pert nose in the air. "But I'll give you a mouse ear if you do!" Her angry tone softened to wistfulness. "It doesn't really matter. He's leaving tonight."

Careful not to let him see the tears shining in her eyes, she opened the door and stepped out onto the widow's walk that surrounded the belvedere. She leaned far out over the wooden balustrade, reaching for the stars.

Uhmmmmm! Mournfully, the hum of the steamboat's whistle floated up to her as it called passengers to board. She whispered to the stars, "The river is taking him away from me."

CHAPTER 4

THE TREACHEROUS CHATTAHOOCHEE! Its red, muddy waters swirled with danger. How many women, Lily wondered, had paced land-locked widow's walks and searched the horizon with anxious eyes as they worried about their seafaring men?

The rumbling blast of the whistle sounded again, drifting through the starlit night to her isolated spot in the high belvedere. Lily could not see the steamboat, but she could visualize the excitement and she longed to be a part of it, to be standing on that deck with Harrison Wingate. Leaning over the wooden balustrade, she imagined herself beside the steadfast man. What fun it would be to take the trip and get to know him better.

"I wish we were going with him."

Lily jumped. She had not realized Foy had stepped out onto the open walkway with her. She looked down at the wistful child. His words, echoing her thoughts, brought her back to reality.

Subdued, she returned to her bedroom. She climbed into her high bed and lay staring up at the airy, white canopy. Usually the cheerful, blue and white room lifted her spirits, but not this time. She had been as carried away by an adolescent dream as young Foy. Mama was right. It was time for her to grow up. This seafaring man was not hers and never could be. There! She had put it plainly to herself. She must forget about Harrison Wingate.

Sighing, she beat her goose-down pillow and turned over with determination to think about the house party and enjoying the courtship of her distant kin from the fabled aristocracy of South Carolina.

Her dreams, however, were of Harrison. He stood on the cold, marble floor of the entrance hall turning his captain's hat in his hands. Hurt etched lines on his face as Emma told him she had gone to Roseland.

Awakening with a start, Lily felt tired, pulled apart by her conflicting emotions. Dressing without her usual care, she wandered listlessly through the garden to the latticed summerhouse. It was a cool and pleasant place. Papa had imported the wicker and rattan furniture from the Orient at her special request when she told him it had become the current rage. Pensively, she sat pulling petals from a rose, rolling them in her fingers, sniffing the sweetness. She glanced up and saw Papa heading toward her. Normally, he would be in his office by now. Had Foy told on her? She tried to mask her apprehension with a smiling greeting.

"Good morning, Papa. You're mighty late going to work. I hope you're not ill?"

"No, no, I'm fine. How's my little girl this morning?" Papa returned too heartily. "Pink is certainly your color." He smiled approvingly and kissed her high-piled curls.

A servant was following behind him with a silver coffee service and a plate of croissants. Seeing that it was a deliberately staged encounter, Lily steeled herself. Tensely, she buttered a flaky roll and sipped coffee, strongly flavored with chicory. Not really hungry, Lily nibbled and chatted about the weather until the servant left them alone.

Papa rubbed his hand over his balding head and cleared his throat. "Your mother wanted me to talk with you."

"Oh, Papa," she wailed.

"Now, now, don't be upset." His voice croaked as it often did when he was agitated. "How do you like your cousin?"

"I've hardly had time to tell. He's very nice, but . . . I certainly don't love him," she finished firmly, jutting out her chin.

Papa set his thin, china cup on the wicker table before he answered. "You will learn to love him as you know him better," he soothed.

"How can I be sure of that with everyone rushing me?" She stuck out her lower lip petulantly.

"I tried to tell your mother that you would rebel at forced arrangements," he sighed. "You must realize that we have your best interests at heart. You are too young to understand yet, but as you see more of life, you will realize the unhappiness that results from marrying out of one's class."

Lily brushed flakes of pastry from the lace at the neckline of her dress and bit her lip thinking, *I'm always too young on the one hand and too old on the other.*

Clare Edwards's head glistened with beads of perspiration standing out on reddening skin. "Don't you remember my cousin Lucinda who ran away with a workman?" He looked at his daughter with loving concern. "Her life ended in bitterness. She was alone, estranged from her family, deserted by her husband. She. . ."

"I wouldn't do that, Papa," she replied in a wilted voice.

"You have social obligations to be met. You will inherit a great many responsibilities."

"Yes, Papa." She bowed her head and clinched fistfuls of rose petals until her fingernails bit into her palms.

"Now, you best go and see your mother." He sighed heavily and patted her awkwardly. "She has a surprise for you—a new frock to take to Roseland."

The carriage turned in from the River Road and stopped at the wide double gates of Roseland Plantation. As the servants rushed to open the white gates, Lily sat back smugly. This plantation was socially prominent throughout the state, and her cousin, who seemed to think nothing here was as grand as in South Carolina, should be impressed. They approached the manor house through a natural woodland of giant water oaks, cedars, and magnolias that still held the last of their huge, waxy-white blossoms and scented the air with heavy perfume. The carriage turned up a broad central walk, two hundred feet long. Sand, white as marble and kept perfectly clear of carriage or horse tread, covered the entire length of this driveway to the white-pillared house that stood resplendent in serene beauty and dignity.

Lily could scarcely contain her excitement as they followed the spirea-garlanded curve of the drive to alight at the wide front steps. General Thomas Flournoy and his wife, who had built this house prior to 1840, graciously greeted the arriving guests. Their daughter, Caroline Elizabeth, rushed out to hug Lily.

"Betty, dear," Lily returned her affectionate greeting, "may I present my cousin Green Bethune from South Carolina."

Betty Flournoy smiled dazzlingly at Green and exclaimed, "Oh, I wonder if you are related to my fiancé, Bethune Beaton McKenzie of Louisville?" She linked her arm in his and ushered him into the house, leaving Lily lagging behind. Miffed, Lily made a show of seeing to Kitty, whom Mama had sent along to take care of her, and to her wardrobe trunk.

"Everybody!" Betty sang out, clapping her hands for attention. "Come meet our guest from South Carolina." She smiled with a smugness that showed she knew this exciting addition would make her house party a huge success.

A cluster of giggling girls turned as one. Their eyes brightened at the perfection of Green's features, and they immediately encircled him.

Green bowed gallantly over each extended hand in turn. He progressed slowly, making polite compliments to each preening girl before he moved to the next.

The faces of the young men, who stood back awaiting their introductions, held mixed emotions. Lily, who was equally unaccustomed to being ignored, watched them in amusement. It was easy to see that some stood in awe of Green's self-assured bearing and stylish clothes while others were plainly jealous of his charm.

That evening when the lively group reassembled after dressing formally for dinner, Green offered Lily his arm and escorted her into the huge dining room. During the first course of hare soup and pheasant soup, Green paid her elaborate compliments; however, by the time the entrées of fillet of hare and curried rabbit were served, everyone was turning to him as the center of attention.

"Miss Betty, you and Mr. McKenzie must include Charleston on your honeymoon tour," he said in his cultured accent. "It is quite the center of our *beau monde*. Our local riches have been compared to Peru. Indeed, it has been said that Charleston is to the North what Lima is to the South: capital of the richest province of their respective hemispheres. There are endless balls and galas—and you must see a Shakespearean drama at the Dock Street Theater." He beamed in turn at each one around the table.

Lily squirmed, slightly embarrassed. When the second course was passed, she sampled only the hot, mixed-game pie.

Individuals began chatting to their partners, but Green turned to Elmira Oaks on the other side of him and told her, "You must visit Middleton Gardens someday. It is quite old and famous." He generously helped himself to the third course, roasted fowl.

Lily turned to Betty's rather plain brother and said, "Josiah Flournoy, you handsome old thing, you broke my heart not coming to my last party. What have you been doing lately?" Through all of the side dishes and elaborate desserts, she kept her back to Green. During the evening as they played charades and dumbo crambo, she continued to ignore Green. Feigning interest in Josiah, she felt a slight pang for toying with him.

The next afternoon, everyone went outdoors to watch as the gentlemen prepared to go fishing. Roseland Plantation boasted of very good fishing in its creek which emptied into the Chattahoochee. As Josiah Flournoy passed out rods and other fine equipment, he explained to Green that the water was very deep and in some places quite wide for a creek.

Green, in turn, explained to him that on his low country plantation, they controlled their water with sluices to flood the earth and grow rice. Lily hated to hear anyone brag, and she was surprised at how well the other men were accepting him, deferring to his superior knowledge and experience.

After bidding the fishermen merry farewells, the girls went back inside to play with cards or hearts as they chose. They chattered incessantly about Betty's upcoming wedding to her young man who was from a Scottish family of high rank. Caught up in the talk of love and romance, Lily began to wonder if marriage to Green might not be fun after all. He was fitting well into her circle of friends. He could show her the new sights she longed to see. Suddenly she realized that Betty was asking her about Green.

"Oh, he's from one of the first families of South Carolina," she replied. Wincing, she knew that she sounded exactly like Mama.

"When did you meet him?"

"Are you in love with him?"

"Are you planning to marry?"

Lily laughed at her friends' eager questions. She tried to smile mysteriously as if she really knew the answers but was not ready to tell. "Well," she temporized, "I'll tell you this much, our families would like to see us married."

The girls pressed her for details, and Lily had difficulty changing the subject.

When the gentlemen returned from their fishing expedition, some of her friends stood back in respect of her half-claim to Green, but Elmira Oaks went straight to him and linked her arm with his. Lily sniffed disdainfully because a lady simply did not make the first advance. The party moved to the cool veranda. Over refreshments the men recounted that the largest bass had gotten away, as usual. While the group laughed over the fish stories and gasped over the killing of a copperhead, Elmira led a willing Green to a double swing at the far end of the porch.

Lily pouted that Green had not come at once to her side. This was supposed to be her courtship, yet he had almost ignored her. Family and friends told Lily she was pretty, but Elmira Oaks was the local reigning beauty. With pearl-like skin, glossy dark hair, and voluptuous figure, Elmira could easily crook her finger at any man. Trying not to look toward the swing, Lily sat gritting her teeth.

"Ohhh, Green, you say the funniest things," Elmira laughed melodiously.

"Well, I'm a member of the Laughing Club," he returned. "No, really, it's one of Charleston's many clubs. But I'm prouder of my membership in the Dueling Society."

"Ohhh, I love a man who lives by the Code of Honor," she squealed.

Encouraged, Green continued. "Our society is modeled after the old London clubs. Admission is granted only to those who have participated in a duel. A man's rank in the organization is based on the number of his encounters."

Lily fanned rapidly with her hand-painted, ivory fan. Glancing over it at Green, she decided that, although a lady did not allow a gentleman to take liberties, perhaps she had been too stringent in cooling his ardor. She had to admit that he far outshone her former beaux.

That evening she spent a great deal of time on her toilette, deciding that she had better give Elmira some competition and make Green notice her. Because Mama had always fussed that she allowed her skin too much sun, she carefully washed her neck and hands with almond meal to whiten them. Next she softened her lips and cheeks with glycerine diluted with rose-water. Frowning at her reflection, she powdered her nose with finely pounded white starch. Kitty was skilled with the curling iron. While she heated it in the fireplace and fashioned Lily's hair into clusters of long curls in back, she whispered excitedly about her budding romance with a strapping stablehand named Lige.

Around them, the bedroom was filled with tinkling giggles and gasps as her friends had their corsets laced to the desired nineteen-inch waist and then fluttered into petticoat after frothy petticoat.

Smiling more confidently now, Lily put on her mother's surprise gift, a creation from the Salon in the Rue de la Paix of Charles Frederick Worth, the English founder of Paris Haute Couture. The lovely emerald silk billowed over her widest, evening hoops. The dainty décolleté bared her creamy shoulders above short puffs of sleeves.

The orchestra was tuning up, and strains of music drifted from the wide back porch as she pulled on her elbow-length gloves and gave herself a final check in the looking glass. Hurrying until she reached the head of the stairs, she paused and drifted down until Green turned his head and saw her. Smiling, he started toward her, and she moved to meet him without further coquettishness.

Green took her hand, and they joined the group lining up to play twistification. They stood in lines of ladies and gentlemen with partners facing. Then the guitar and fiddle commenced a lively tune. The end couple bowed and clasped both hands as they swung each other around. Still swirling, they grasped the hands of the next in line and continued to swing each person until they reached the end of the line. When their turn came, Lily returned the squeeze of Green's fingers; however, she smiled dazzlingly at each man who swung her down the line. It would not hurt to make Green jealous, too. As she stood panting, waiting for her turn to come as the lines twisted and undulated again and again, Lily was unsure whether her breathlessness came from keeping time to the music or from Green's intimate glances and the pressure of his hands whenever they rejoined as partners.

Twistification was considered a game allowed to those whose churches might turn them out for dancing. Some dances and other games followed.

Resting between sets, the couples strolled the geometric patterns of the formal garden paths. The fragrance of hundreds of roses filled the soft, June night. Marechal Neil, La France, and the dainty buds of Devoniensis were the favorites that caused the girls to stop, bend over the clipped boxwood edging, and breathe deeply. Rambling roses draped the fence at the perimeter of the garden. The heady fragrance seemed to pulse to the muted beat of the music. Here and there a large boxwood or American holly cast a secluded shadow, and marble benches offered a spot to rest; however, the young people were never far from the watchful eyes of their chaperones. Green's manner toward her had changed. Responding to her bid for his attention, he made every effort to charm and court her. When he led her through the pergola, a long procession of columns screened by a web of climbing roses, she made only a weak protest as he stole a kiss beneath the romantic bower.

After a light, midnight supper of chicken salad, ham, cakes, jellies, and meringues, the dancing continued until three in the morning. Then the groups returned to their various guest quarters. The girls in Lily's room whispered until dawn streaked the sky, and Lily had no chance to sort out her feelings for her suitor.

Before departing for home after brunch the next day, the couples promenaded to Roseland's private landing on a curve of the Chattahoochee. They stood laughing and chatting as they watched the farmhands bringing peaches, vegetables, and meats to be loaded aboard the steamboat for its dining room.

Uhmmm! The whistle of the steamboat around the bend vibrated against Lily's ribs. She held her breath. Uh-Uh-Uhmm! It was not the signal for the *Wave*, but she stood on tiptoe to see.

Green reached for her hand. "How would you like to take a grand tour?"

Lily looked at him in surprise. Was he suggesting they begin thinking of a honeymoon tour? Although his voice was bantering, he was gazing at her quite seriously.

"I—don't know," she faltered, realizing that he had misread her excitement.

"We could sail to Charleston and New York City, and then go to Saratoga and Newport if you like."

"That—would be lovely," she murmured hesitantly. Turning toward the river, she lowered her parasol so that he could not see her face. She had told herself that she had grown up, that she was ready to take her place in society.

The long, flat boat floated alongside, and everyone waved and called out gaily. Lily's hand barely moved, and she said nothing as her eyes sought the vessel, hoping she had mistaken the signal. A huge wheel churned water at the stern. Harrison's steamer had a sidewheel. Would she ever again hear a steamboat's whistle or smell the smoke without searching for Harrison Wingate's face?

Back home at Barbour Hall, Lily rushed upstairs to find Emma to share the fun of the house party and the details of Betty Flournoy's upcoming wedding. Emma sat sewing in her favorite spot, the sitting room at the front of the hall. This was the only small room in the house, and both girls enjoyed its intimacy when the sliding doors shut it off from the rest of the hall.

Smiling and nodding Emma listened patiently to Lily's excited tale. When Lily paused for breath at last, Emma spoke quietly, "Harrison Wingate came soon after you left."

Lily's dark eyes widened and her animated face became solemn. "Was he hurt at my not being here?"

"Well, he's so quiet and dignified," Emma returned, looking at her seriously, "and he doesn't say very much. We had a very nice visit though. . . ." Her voice trailed away.

Lily looked at her aunt who obviously had more to say. Emma, however, compressed her lips and made a show of searching for thread in the black japanned papier-maché sewing stand by her chair. Lily sat down on the window seat and leaned far out onto the small circular balcony that decorated the porch roof above the entrance doors of the house. She gazed across the grounds that were dappled with sunlight and shade and struggled with the emotions that had sprung up at Emma's words. Emma always listened when Lily spilled out the inmost feelings of her heart; however, she concealed her own desires beneath a placid face and averted eyes. Emma seemed resigned to spinsterhood, but she must long for a better life than she had. Lily glanced back at her through the curtain of her blowing hair, but she could see no emotion revealed. If Emma and Harrison fell in love and she married Green, everyone should be happy. . . .Then, why was she fighting so hard to keep back the tears?

She wanted to run out into the garden, to scream and cry like a child. Instead, she concealed her tears and went quietly to her room. She had been telling herself she only wanted the captain for a friend. She enjoyed his lively conversation that recognized her own bright mind. Because she approached life with intense convictions about everything, Harrison's amusing lightness relaxed her tensions. Suddenly she knew that she wanted more than passing friendship from Harrison Wingate.

Exhaustion overwhelmed her. Stepping out of her crinoline, she climbed into her bed and hugged herself into a tight little knot of despair. Green would be pressing her soon for an engagement. She knew she must do what everyone was expecting of her. If she did not give him a definite answer, he would be turning to other fields. Harrison's face floated before her, and the thought of his smiles turned upon another, left her aching. She had no one to advise her now. She was bereft of her confidante.

Betty Flournoy's wedding day was as perfect as only a clear summer day can be. As Lily and Green approached the church, she was proud of her escort's appearance. A high top hat and thin walking stick added to his elegance.

Because the past few weeks since the house party had been such a busy social whirl, Lily had been able to stave off an official engagement; however, she had almost resigned herself to it.

The line of carriages stopping at the church stretched well down the street. Too excited to sit still, Lily suggested that they alight from the carriage and walk the rest of the way.

"Oh, look, Green," she plucked at his sleeve. "I've never seen anything more wonderful!"

She directed his gaze to a strange sight back down the street. An old man, who was apparently quite helpless, sat in a large chair on wheels that was being pulled along by a goat.

"Let's go chat with him and give him some money," she said eagerly.

"No, my sweet, I can't have you looking on such ugliness," Green replied with finality. Taking her elbow, he turned her toward the church.

Lily glanced back over her shoulder. Smiling at the ingenious man, she wished she could do more.

"Lily, Lily," the other bridesmaids called nervously.

She hurried to join them. Swelling music stirred her heart as the bevy of bridesmaids fluttered down the aisle. As they turned and caught sight of the lovely bride in her pearl-encrusted, white satin, each girl drew breath as one. Lily's misty eyes sought Green's as she consented to herself to smile a promise to him. He was sweet and protective of her, she realized. Soon she too would be dressed in white satin. She should make the best of a situation she could not change.

As the organ trumpeted the single notes and then crashed into the stirring chords of Mendelssohn's "Wedding March from a Midsummer Night's Dream," Lily's feet danced to the trills of the recessional. Her heart filled with the music and she moved to Green's side.

With her decision made, she happily participated in all of the wedding festivities and returned home in high spirits.

As she swirled through the double entrance doors of Barbour Hall, she glimpsed a letter waiting on the card tray. With a shuddering sigh she recognized the seal on it as being the dove insignia from the *Wave*. Her fingers shook as she reached for it only to draw back quickly.

It was addressed to Emma.

CHAPTER 5

THE LETTER SEEMED TO MOVE, to taunt her. Lily's trembling fingers flew to her face in a vain effort to hide her emotions. Pleading extreme weariness, she escaped to her room.

She stood at the long window looking out at the stars as they began to twinkle. She must pull herself together and be pleased for Emma. After all, she had Green. He wanted to make her happy, to shield her from the ugliness of life.

Lily could not seem to make a formal petition, yet her thoughts meshed with snatches of prayer. She did not want a perpetual-house-party life, much as she enjoyed fun. She loved attending church and was not pleased that Green usually pled too much business to accompany her. She always left worship services inspired that Jesus had saved her to serve. She did not want to turn away from the twisted old men and goats of life; she wanted to help.

Suddenly she realized that she did not really love

Green. She had been caught up in the romance of the moment at the wedding. She knew that Papa was right that sometimes love grew and flowered after marriage, but now she doubted that would be the case if she married Green. He was handsome. Charming. Perhaps the passion of which she knew so little might flourish for a season, but deep within her she knew they would never be one in mind and spirit.

Sadly, she began to take off her wedding finery.

The door opened slowly and Emma came in clutching the letter to her chest with both hands. The willowy girl leaned against the doorjamb as if she might fall without support. Her face pinched with doubt, she said, "I just don't know what to do."

Lily lifted pain-filled eyes to her friend and waited.

"I know I shouldn't tell you. I should burn this letter and never tell you. Your mother will never forgive me." She sat down in the rocking chair and began to cry softly.

Tortured by the excruciatingly drawn out revelation, Lily patted her hand and made soothing sounds she did not feel.

"Here." Emma thrust the letter toward her. "Read it."

Lily recoiled. She would be loving. She would be pleasant. But she could not read Harrison's words of love to Emma.

"Read it," she repeated. "It's yours."

"Mine? I don't understand."

"Read it," she said again as if to a stupid child. "You'll understand."

June 12, 1858

Apalachicola, Florida

Amie De Mon Coeur,

May I call you that, my darling Lily? I have sent this by your, or may I say our, dear friend Emma, in order not to embarrass you if my love for you is not requited. I was devastated that I missed seeing you, but I quite unburdened my heart to Emma! From the first moment I saw the compassion on your face as you watched the scene on the steamer from beneath your parasol, I have loved you. I dare not hope that you love me as I love you, but it would give me such joy if you would correspond with me so that we can get to know each other better. Send a letter by Julian McKenzie aboard the *Laura* and he will get it to me.

I anxiously await hearing from you. I do not mean to practice a deception upon your parents, but Emma agreed to accept a first letter until I could be certain of your feelings for me. By her nervousness in the matter, I judge that she fears this may be contrary to her duties as your chaperone, but as I said, she is friend to both of us.

Please do not disappoint me.

Good night. God bless you.

Harrison Wingate

Lily looked up from the letter with shining eyes. "Oh, Emma, thank you so much. I know you risked Mama's ire. And she treats you terribly now."

"Yes. Perhaps that's why I risked this letter," Emma sighed. "Oh, no, I don't mean to spite her," she added quickly. "She is kind to give me a home. But her domineering ways have made my life so miserable that I had to let you decide for yourself if you would follow your heart." She clutched and unclutched her hands in a nervous gesture that made her seem far older than her twenty-five years. "I did not follow mine."

"I've never known why you didn't marry," Lily said softly. "You are the sweetest person I've ever known—and so lovely." She stood over her friend and patted her bowed head of honey-colored hair.

Emma smiled up at her with a look of infinite sadness in her pale blue eyes. "I was very much in love with a young man who asked for my hand. My grandfather refused to allow the marriage because he was not of our faith."

"Well, Harrison is a Christian with a faith even stronger than my own. But would Papa and Mama ever accept him? Papa might, but Mama is so set on Green. . . ."

"What about Green? Do you love him at all?"

"He made me jealous," she laughed sheepishly, "and I thought perhaps I did. The simplest solution to my problems would be to marry him. I want to obey my parents, and life would follow the pattern I'm accustomed to – I can't imagine what sort of life I'd have with Harrison . . ." She dropped her head in her hands.

Emma nodded and said nothing.

Lily reached for the letter again and held it to her cheek. "But wouldn't it be exciting . . ." she sighed.

"You'll answer the letter then?"

"Yes. Whatever the outcome, I'll answer the letter. Even if I never see him again, I'll answer the letter!"

Lily spent a restless night as her tired body pulled toward sleep and her excited mind composed and recomposed her letter.

In the morning, she took her brass-bound, rosewood lap desk to the summerhouse. As she unfolded the writing slope, the ardent letters she had envisioned in the night embarrassed her. She thought for a long time before she dipped her pen in the crystal inkwell and began carefully.

June 21, 1858

Eufaula, Alabama

Dear Captain Wingate,

I received your letter and was delighted to hear from you. I would enjoy corresponding with you and hearing about your exciting travels.

I am very sorry that I had gone to Roseland when you returned. The house party served well to entertain my visiting cousin and give me a chance to enjoy seeing Betty Flournoy before her marriage. Her lovely wedding was yesterday. I am certain you would not be interested in that, but I did see something on the way that you would have appreciated. A crippled old man who had rebelled at being bedridden was moving smartly along in a chair on wheels pulled by a goat. How is that for spirit?

Wind ruffled her paper. The open lattice of the summerhouse, partially roofed with swags of wisteria, filtered the sunlight but invited every breeze. Happily Lily looked up from her writing. With a green blur of wings, a hummingbird hovered over a large buddelia. The glory of its tiny being filled her with longing to be near Harrison once again, to absorb the pleasure in the small things of life that he exuded. She wanted to pour out her heart to him, but she feared being unmaidenly. She contented herself with writing a chatty letter and signed it, "Yours, Lily."

As the summer days sizzled by, Lily drifted in a daze. Chiding herself for constantly daydreaming of Harrison and watching for a letter from him, she was relieved when business took the usually indolent Green by stagecoach to Tuskegee. Her nerves had barely relaxed before they stretched taut again. Mama began to talk about taking a trip to Columbus to visit her sister who had an exceedingly fine dressmaker. Fearing Harrison might return and knowing Mama had in mind beginning a trousseau, Lily tried to discourage her. Although no one had verbally set a deadline for her, she sensed pressure from all sides to announce an engagement.

Lily and Emma descended the stairs early one morning bound for a walk to the Chewalla bridge. They were hurrying, both to leave before the day became too hot and to escape the scrutiny of Cordelia Edwards. As they slipped softly across the marble floor, the butler placed a letter on the card tray. It bore Emma's name, but a brief nod from her aunt made Lily scoop it up, clutch it to her heart, and run across the lawn like a child at play. Plopping down behind a large bush with her skirt mushrooming around her, she ripped open the letter.

Smith's Bend, Alabama

Dear Lily,

The *Wave* will leave here shortly and it's headed your way! Please, please be there this time. I received your letter with joy. Even though you spoke no words of love for me, I could feel it between the lines. I will be in Eufaula only briefly this trip for the bulk of my load must get directly to Columbus. I must see you. Even if a smile across the water is all you can give, please be there. We should arrive on the tenth of July.

I love you dearly,

Harrison Wingate

Excuse this pencil note. I am writing hurriedly on an old sideboard to get this off to you.

Lily's footsteps danced along the way to Chewalla bridge and Emma nervously clutched her fists against her chest as she listened to the girl's daring plan to board Harrison's steamer.

Uhmmmmm! Uhmmmmm!

The steamboat's whistle aroused Lily from her sleep. She sat bolt upright in the darkness. Jumping off the high bed, she dressed quickly. It had been simple to agree with Mama to take the next steamboat to Columbus to visit with her sister; however, the boat had not arrived that evening as expected. Everyone had finally despaired of the steamer docking and retired for the night. Now, summoned by the wheeting whistle, they hurried to the waterfront.

Burning torches illuminated the scene. Lily pranced along as they alighted from the carriage and joined the others going aboard for Columbus. Cordelia Edwards never noticed details of things she considered beneath her; consequently, she had not guessed that Harrison Wingate was master of this steamboat.

They hastened past the brick warehouse onto the wharf that was overflowing with freight. The night air rang with shouts and laughter as the stevedores hurried to unload the steamboat. Excitedly, Lily eyed the long train of wagons, sent by merchants at Clayton, Ozark, and Abbeville, waiting to haul out the freight.

As soon as they had gone up the gangway, Mrs. Edwards, professing that she felt in a stupor from being awakened, went to her cabin to bed. Giving in to Lily's pleading to stay up a little while, she left her daughter in Emma's care.

The girls stayed on the upper deck and watched the

process of unloading and loading. Lily's cheeks flushed with excitement as she caught glimpses of Harrison. He had greeted them all briefly, but had immediately returned to his work.

At last the shouts of the roustabouts stilled, the whistle stopped blasting, and the steamer glided into the dark silent river. The only sound was the water wheel's slow swish, swish, swish.

The pounding of Lily's heart slowed to a peaceful rhythm, and she seemed to stop breathing as she watched the quiet man moving steadily along the deck toward her. Emma drifted away to a chair in the shadow of the staterooms.

"I'm sorry I've been so busy since you all came aboard," Harrison smiled down at her as he joined her at the rail. "That you're going with me is more than I dared dream."

"I'm afraid I've been rather devious," she confessed, lowering her lashes shyly. "I let Mama think it coincidence that this was your boat."

Harrison's deep voice chuckled. "I thought she was surprised to see me."

"She'd been wanting to visit a dressmaker and . . ." she hesitated, remembering the purpose of seeing the seamstress. She wished that time could stand as still as the steamer seemed to be doing; but as moonlight played over the shore, the dark bank seemed to move by and she knew that she could not remain a belle juggling suitors. All artifice vanished as she freed her mind and soul. She lifted wide, honest eyes to his face, and stood waiting, awash with moonglow.

"Oh, Lily," Harrison's laughter stilled. Solemnly, he moved nearer, and his hands hovered close to her shoulders, then dropped to the rail. "You've made me so happy—coming with me. I. . . ."

Motionless, scarcely daring to believe the love she saw shining in his eyes, she matched his gaze. Her arms tingled even though his fingers had not quite touched her. Standing so close, breathing the same air he was breathing, she knew he was sharing the same wonder of discovered love. "Harrison," she sighed, as he lifted her hands and tenderly kissed her fingertips.

"You're the loveliest, most beautiful. . . ." He looked down at her as if he must make up for the hours that had been so empty away from each other. He caressed her dark hair as it floated on the summer breeze.

Tenderness welled up within her and spilled over as soft laughter.

Gently, he brushed her a kiss. She caught her breath with a tremulous sigh.

"Lily!" A hiss sounded from Emma who had moved down the deck toward them. "Lily, we'd best get to our cabin. Your mother might awaken."

"All right, Emma," she called softly and moved reluctantly away from Harrison who continued to hold her outstretched hand.

"Until tomorrow," he promised, bending his dark head to kiss her fingertips one last time.

Smiling back at Harrison, she allowed Emma to lead her toward the staterooms that stretched three fourths of the length of the boat. They shared the small room next to Mama's, and they opened the door from the deck stealthily lest they wake her.

"Lily," Emma hissed again, "I'm afraid."

"Of what?" asked Lily in surprise.

"Shhh. Don't let your mother hear. I'm afraid you're heading for trouble. I should never have helped you deceive her."

"I haven't told her any lies. . . ."

"No, but you didn't tell her Captain Wingate would be on this run."

"Really now," Lily struggled out of her hooped skirt, "I couldn't be sure anything would come of it. He might ask lots of girls to ride, and . . ." she faltered.

"Exactly! You don't know what sort of man he is." Emma's blue eyes held deep concern.

"I think I do," Lily replied with quiet assurance.

"But what do you know about him? Has he told you anything about his background?"

"No, but—"

"Well?"

"He doesn't talk about himself all the time like Green does." Lily was tired now, petulant. "He talks about the present—vital things. Oh, Emma, you're not going to make me doubt him. Now, go to sleep," she said soothlingly. "We'll see what tomorrow brings."

Lily lay in her bunk, smiling at the ceiling, warmed by the remembered tenderness of Harrison's kiss. She could hardly wait for morning.

Breakfast would be served on tables set up in the center hallway between the two rows of staterooms, but Lily chose to walk around the rail even though the room opened onto the hall. She was not disappointed; Harrison stood on deck. He smiled and waved, but he was busy directing a stop at a plantation landing to take on food supplies and cord wood for fuel. It was this fat pine and rosin that caused the smokestacks to belch such black smoke. Lily could glimpse a stately mansion on the hill overlooking the muddy water.

Looking down, Lily laughed at a brown mother duck bustling along with five fuzzy babies bobbing intently behind her in a golden-headed knot. Blending into a brown rock, a crowd of turtles sunned lazily.

Every spattering drop of the river sustained some form of life. From a rock out-cropping, fern fronds dipped lacy fingers. Yellows, whites, and blues of wildflowers dotted tiny clods of earth. They were closely attended by huge, black bees and brilliant butterflies. A spider crocheted a sparkling web. Drinking in the beauty, Lily felt she might burst with happiness. The steamboat moved back into the channel of the river that was at once peaceful, smooth, sparkling, swirling, eddying. Lifting her eyes toward the eastern shore, Lily marveled at the beauty of maple leaves translucent with sunlight. As the boat labored upstream, the soft, early morning rays filtered and patterned through tall trees laced with vines that swayed and danced to the orchestration of the songbirds. Lily's heart swelled with the music, and she offered up a thankful prayer to the Creator.

Suddenly famished, she went inside to eat. The interior of the boat was well appointed. Chandeliers reflected back from mirrors and ornamented spittoons. Lily smiled approvingly at Harrison's use of greenery, and she noted as she walked down the carpeted passageway, that the boat was well kept. The fifty passengers were served in two sittings. Lily joined the second group and ate a bountiful breakfast.

Mama went with a friend to the ladies saloon to chat. Delighted that she had escaped Mama's scrutiny, Lily stepped back into the sunshine, filled with anticipation. Emma followed her.

"Morning, ladies," Captain Wingate tipped his hat politely as he joined them. "The banks are so pretty along here that I always wish I could sit on them awhile and throw out a line to a bass or crappie." He pointed to the steep slanted bank on the Georgia side. On the west, Alabama rose a sheer bluff. "And the catfish, here—ah," he kissed his fingertips and gestured lavishly, "the best you've ever tasted!"

Lily had never cared for fishing, but felt anything would be fun with Harrison. She wanted to tell him so. She winked at Emma and motioned with a nod.

Remaining steadfastly in her position as chaperone, Emma returned a frown. "Oh, look," she shivered and pointed as two tremendous alligators slid off a sand bar with a foghorn-like bellow at the approach of the boat.

Harrison accepted Emma's presence pleasantly and he entertained them both, laughing and joking and pointing out landmarks along the steep banks. Suddenly the river narrowed, deepened. Oaks shouldered poplars and gums as they pushed to the water's edge. Rushing to meet the steamboat through this green-velvet canyon, the Chattahoochee, revealing itself a little at a time, tempting them toward new delights around the bend always just ahead, flowed clear, dark, cool.

Breaking the spell, a call from the mate, Captain Allen, summoned Harrison. With a flurry of excitement, the passengers moved around the deck toward the shouting.

A slow-going raft of logs lashed together floated downstream just ahead of the unwieldy steamboat. A small tent on the raft sheltered the owner who had chosen this method of marketing his logs. The man waved and motioned apologetically, but he could do little to move from the ship's path.

Lily beamed with pride as Harrison, perfectly calm in the midst of everyone's agitation, maneuvered his ship safely past the raft.

When Harrison rejoined them he shrugged off the excitement. "Rafts do make our passage difficult, but these men make a handsome profit on their lumber if they can get it safely downstream to a good market." He smiled down at her and there was a boyish pride and enthusiasm in his eyes as he asked, "Would you like to tour the steamer?"

"I'd love to," exclaimed Lily. Giving them this time together Emma took a seat in a deck chair.

Foy, however, popped up from nowhere. Ignoring Lily's glaring, he asked, "May I go?"

"Certainly son, glad to have you," Harrison said cordially.

The trio climbed to the hurricane deck, a short section of rooms between the smokestacks. "This is where the officers live," Captain Wingate explained. "Henry Shreve, a pioneer in steamboating named the rooms of his boats for individual states, hence the term 'stateroom'. Many people call this deck the Texas ever since Texas entered the Union as the biggest state of all."

Foy's rosy cheeks glowed with excitement. Lily peeped shyly into the captain's quarters and tried to maintain dignity, but she was almost as excited as her little brother when they climbed to the small glassed-in pilothouse. From here, they could look beyond the fluttering flags to the treetops along the banks or scan far down the river. With a touch of arrogance, the pilot showed them how he made decisions and snapped orders to the engineer and his helpers far below. Of course, Foy wanted to see the huge furnaces being fed. Lily waited for them in a deck chair.

She had never enjoyed anything as much as she enjoyed being with Harrison and watching him move about in his world. She was sorry that Columbus was only eighty-five miles from Eufaula and they were due to land there at two o'clock that afternoon. When would she ever see Harrison again?

They had only gone a few miles when the river made a decided turn south.

Suddenly the boat stopped with a resounding thud. Passengers caught off guard because of the normally smooth sailing, fell sprawling about the deck. Harrison ran to see what debris had been struck. Worse than mere debris, the boat had hit the sand bar at Francis Bend. Like a great mermaid stretching languorously with sunlight glittering off of pure white skin, the bar had lured many ill-fated boats.

When inspection showed that the *Wave* had not torn a hole in her hull but was firmly grounded, Lily whispered to Emma with twinkling eyes, "What a delightful disaster."

Two in the afternoon passed. Lily leaned over the rail, grinning mischievously, happy that all of the workmen's efforts to dislodge the craft were to no avail. As the sun began sinking in a cloud over the water, a mist settled in. Streaks of pinks and golds reflected over and again, sparkling, drifting, lifting in gentle waves. Smiling, Lily went to her cabin.

She emerged wearing cream colored mousseline de

soie. Soft swags around the hem and across the shoulders and bodice were caught up with currant-red velvet ribbons.

Catching sight of her, Harrison motioned to the Italian orchestra on the hurricane deck. Soft strains of music swirled around them as they danced in the twilight. As the moonlight turned the sand bar to softly gleaming silver, other passengers came on deck and joined the dancing; but Lily felt she and Harrison were floating on a cloud, alone.

Dinner was a festive affair. Because they were seated with the captain, Lily eyed her mother apprehensively. Surprisingly, Cordelia Edwards was beaming. Lily realized that Mama quite expected her to be the belle of any situation, and, here, the dashing captain was the one to whom all eyes turned. As many gentlemen claimed her for the dancing that followed the elaborate meal, Mama could not know that Lily glowed because she was falling in love.

The next day, the steamer remained firmly grounded. Food supplies were slightly depleted, but gaiety ran high; and everyone gorged on a load of fresh pineapple. Banjo picking added to the merriment as passengers, who had by now become friends, lounged in deck chairs, chatting. It was cool on deck. The banks on both sides were dense woodland thickly hung with swaying swags of Spanish moss. In Lily's lively imagination, the gay shrouds became Indian ghosts singing with the voice of the wind in the pines. The boat was stopped in full view of an ancient Indian mound, a great oblong shape of red clay some thirteen feet to its flat summit and a hundred feet in diameter. The passengers speculated about the mysteries of the mound.

When Harrison climbed down again to the sand bar, Lily moved to the rail to watch. The eight acres of deep sand were heavily populated with seiners as well as with workmen from the *Wave*. Lily watched them chain their fish baskets to stakes on the sand bar, swim out into the yellow water with their seines, and return with a catch of garfish, carp, cat, and suckers.

A cheer went up. The sweating workmen had freed the vessel at last. Lily sighed in disappointment; however, it was nearly night, and she could enjoy one last evening with Harrison.

Beneath the stars, they danced once more to the singing violins. Spinning with happiness, she did not realize at first that he was whirling her away from the group.

"My lovely Lily, *Je t'aime*," Harrison whispered against her hair. Taking both her hands in his, he drew back and looked into her eyes. "I've loved you from the first moment I saw you. Each glimpse of you makes me love you more. Dare I hope that you can learn to love me?"

"Yes, Harrison," she whispered softly. "I do love you, oh, I do!"

Placing his arm around her shoulder, he guided her further along the rail to a secluded spot. Cupping her face with a strong hand, he tilted her head and bent down to kiss her tenderly. Shyly, she accepted his kiss. Opening her eyes slowly, wondrously, she looked up at him. The depth of his love was plainly read on his candid face. Moonlight, softly caressing the water surrounding them, reflected in her dark, shining eyes. She entwined her slender arms about his neck.

"I love you, Harrison, and I always will."

He swept her into his arms. She responded to the desire of his kisses until at last, remembering decorum, she eased away.

"I don't mean to rush you, Lily," Harrison said. "I know you deserve a long and proper courtship, but for now I must stay with the steamship line. If I were still on the family plantation, I would perhaps have proper time." He laughed and shook his head. "No, I could never wait for you. I want you to be mine immediately. May I ask your father for your hand?"

"Yes, yes," she breathed. "When we get back to Eufaula, speak to Papa. Don't let on to Mama, now."

Harrison nodded and reached to draw her close again.

Lily awakened early the next morning, and slipped out to the mist-shrouded deck. The dark forest shimmered, blurred. Gradually, she focused on two black, curious eyes. Alert ears pointed upward, quivering. With a sudden flip of a white tail, the deer bounded away. Enchanted, she peered closer and saw an entire deer family feeding quietly, moving silently through the woodland. Led by a quarrelsome gobbler, a flock of wild turkeys jerked and bobbed its way to a rock-bound pool. A fat white-breasted gray bird dipped its beak quickly and scurried out of their way.

A hand grasped Lily's shoulder and she turned to find her mother's wary eye upon her. Mrs. Edwards insisted she come in out of the dampness, and they went into the ladies saloon together. It was a large and lovely room dominated by a Chickering grand piano in one corner. Small writing desks lined the windows. Potted palms and ferns formed the chairs into cozy groupings. Mrs. Edwards selected a large rocker, and

Lily took a stool beside her. Dutifully, she began to read the Bible aloud as Cordelia Edwards directed her. Mama reared back smiling and nodding with pleasure as others came in and saw her daughter respectfully at her feet.

They had come to the Book of Ruth. Lily began by merely speaking the words. Gradually, the story gripped her attention. When she came to the sixteenth verse of chapter one and read in her Bible ". . .for whither thou goest, I will go; and where thou lodgest, I will lodge: thy people shall be my people, and thy God my God," the words began to sing. The beautiful love story spoke to her heart and reinforced her joy in her decision to marry Harrison. Breakfast was announced. She put the Bible aside reluctantly, wanting to read about the marriage of Ruth and Boaz. Wistfully, she remembered that they had had Naomi's blessing. She wished that her mother was the sort of woman with whom she could share the deep convictions which were growing in her heart.

After breakfast, the gentlemen passengers came in and everyone engaged in pleasant conversation. Lily listened with half an ear, frustrated because rain kept her from sitting on deck where she might watch Harrison. During a break in the clouds, she took a stroll and had a brief moment with him.

"Lily, dearest, I'll be staying in Columbus for a few days. You will be going back with me on Monday, won't you?" Harrison asked with anxious eyes.

"Yes," she wiped a spatter of rain from her cheek and smiled radiantly. "Mama never stays away from Papa for very long. I can hardly wait 'til Monday."

"I don't want to wait. Can't I call on you at your aunt's house?"

Lily gripped the wet rail. "Oh, I want to see you! I do. But Mama would be terribly angry if I crossed her in front of her sister. I'm just afraid—"

"Captain Wingate," the mate stepped up deferentially, "we're approaching Columbus."

Distractedly, Wingate nodded to him and searched Lily's face for an answer.

Biting her lip, Lily hesitated. The swishing of the giant sidewheel filled her ears, and her stomach churned as she looked at the foaming wake behind it. In the joy of finding mutual love, she had been growing up, changing; but, suddenly panic seized her. "You'd better not come," she whispered miserably.

A gust of wind covered her with dirty water from the roof. Harrison Wingate was walking away from her toward duty. With dampened spirits and misty eyes, she shuddered with the certainty that Mama would never change.

CHAPTER 6

"LILY!" MAMA'S VOICE SUMMONED HER. "Stop day-dreaming and get your things together. We must hurry and quit the boat before the storm breaks."

Dazed, Lily turned. The sun was blazing down upon her. Beads of perspiration stood out on her forehead. She had forgotten to put on her hat, again. Looking up, she saw an ominous black cloud north of the spot where Cordelia Edwards stood commandingly.

"Yes, ma'am," she sighed.

Their relatives were waving from the wharf. Emma tugged at her arm and pulled her toward the gangway. Clanging bells and shrieking whistles echoed in her head. She clenched her teeth and let the frenzy of humanity swirl around her.

Looking back over her shoulder, she searched for Harrison. He stood on the top deck. His seeking eyes found hers, and their gaze spanned the distance. For one long moment, sound ceased. Peace filled her heart as they spoke eloquent, if silent, words across the intervening water.

Gashing across the sky, lightning seemed to open the sagging bottom of a thunderhead releasing a torrent of rain. They ran toward the carriage. Emma and Cordelia kept jumping nervously because of the frightening fireworks of the July thunderstorm, but Lily scarcely noticed. Huddled in a corner, she wrapped herself in dreams of Harrison until they reached Aunt Laurie's handsome, brick house.

The rest of the family met them on the veranda, set off by exquisite iron grill work, and Lily did not have another quiet moment.

As soon as they could change their wet clothing for afternoon frocks, they came downstairs to the parlor where Aunt Laurie had spread a sumptuous tea for friends who had assembled to greet them. Cousin Octavia was called upon to perform on the piano. Gracefully, she lifted her hoop over the red velvet stool and seated herself with her skirt billowing completely around it. Lily, who always moved too quickly for this type of maneuver and made her hoop fly up in back, was glad that she was only requested to stand beside the square, grand piano and sing.

When at last the girls had a chance to sit together on one of the winged love seats, Octavia whispered, "I can't wait to hear about your beau." A frown creased her sweet, round face and she tossed her corn-shuck hair at the wry expression this brought to Lily's face. She continued in a puzzled voice, "One time I look at you, you're terrible unhappy and the next minute you're grinning like a cow eating briars."

Lily laughed. She had always liked her plump-cheeked cousin; however, she was afraid to confide in her for fear she would tell Aunt Laurie.

The next morning, Lily was fitted by the dressmaker. As dainty undergarments, gowns and peignoirs took shape, everyone laughed and teased her about being a blushing bride. Guiltily, Lily knew her red cheeks and subdued mien came from concealing the fact that she intended Harrison, not Green, to become her groom.

Mama bragged to her sister about Green. Haughtily, she suggested that it was certainly time for Laurie to make a match for Octavia; although, she doubted that she could find a suitor with equal financial and social aspects for bringing up her grandchildren. Her words rasped Lily's nerves.

In the flurry of shopping trips and social calls, she finally pulled Mrs. Edwards aside. "Please, let me talk with you, Mama," she begged. "I just don't love Green. I don't want to marry—"

"Nonsense!" Cordelia Edwards patted her hand, smiling absently. "Affection will come." She brushed her aside. "Hurry and get ready, baby, it's time for the party."

The sweltering July days were frequently punctuated with violent thunderstorms, and the streets were becoming muddy rivers. Octavia insisted, however, that she must show Lily the Paper Factory on Rock Island. Emma did not wish to go so they set off with Kitty in attendance.

As the carriage rolled along the street which paralleled the river, Octavia pointed out the many beautiful homes. "That one has a patriotic flare," she said, pointing to a Greek revival mansion. "Its eleven columns and two pilasters represent the thirteen original colonies."

"That's nice," murmured Lily absently, lost in the

pleasant pain of loving Harrison but being separated from him. She tried to imagine that he was beside her, marveling at the individualistic architecture along this street. With him, it would not be a boring blur. Every detail would become exciting.

Octavia eyed her, but said nothing more as they rode through the city of Columbus, Georgia, and out into the country.

Lily found the manufacture of paper to be quite a curiosity. As she listened attentively to the gentleman who conducted the tour, she thought that Harrison would find this interesting, too.

Reverberating thunder signaled another storm. Lily gnawed her thumb as they waited it out. Standing, looking at the rain, she began to tremble. If only Mama could see how alike she and Harrison were in mind and heart, surely she would accept him. The storm ended as abruptly as it had begun, and the girls hurried to the carriage. Lily splattered a swath of red mud across her skirt, and her face clouded. They climbed into the carriage, but it would not budge.

"Ma'am," said their driver, "the wheels are firmly mired."

With a long, shuddering sigh, Lily released her pent up emotions and began to sob uncontrollably.

Her cousin looked at her in surprise. "This isn't like you, Lily! The driver can attend to it. What's the matter with you?"

"Oh, Octavia," she gulped. "I'm so much in love."

"Is that all?" Octavia laughed. "That's wonderful. It's marvelous when one can find a love match within the bounds of class."

Lily sobbed harder. As the driver went for assistance in getting the carriage from the muddy bog, she confessed her dilemma.

Shocked, her cheeks quivering, Octavia listened. Nervously chewing a lock of her long hair, she said in a hoarse whisper, "You know girls like us can't marry without our mother's consent."

Lily nodded miserably.

"And what will you tell Green?" Octavia's eyes widened with fear. "From what you've told me of him, he won't take it lightly!"

Shaking her dark head in despair, Lily sobbed until she felt sick and weak.

Sunday morning they attended worship service. Looking hopefully across the gas-lit sanctuary Lily twisted this way and that, craning to see each face. She whispered to Octavia, "I do wish I'd told Harrison which church we'd attend so you could, at least, have seen him."

As the choir marched in filling the building with voices lifted in praise, Lily's tense shoulders relaxed. Laying aside her problems and opening her heart, she let the Spirit of the Lord fill her through the music and the reading of the Scripture. Although the sermon seemed unrelated to her situation, a word here, a phrase there, spoke to her with God's promise that the way might be difficult but He would go with her. Leaving the church with joy and strength renewed, she wished that she could communicate her security of salvation to Emma. The dear, sweet girl had made an excuse not to come, as she often did. She seemed to believe that behaving piously and attending church occasionally were simply more duties she had to perform.

When the family left the church, they decided to ride out to look at the Chattahoochee. It was rising rapidly from the constant storms. Columbus was situated on the fall line separating their gentle land in the Gulf Coastal Plain from the swiftly rising Piedmont. Here the river foamed over rocky falls. Watching the patterning of lights and shadows undulating over the pinks, golds, browns, and whites of the rocks and reflecting in the shoals clearly showed why the Creek Indians had named it *chatta*, meaning stones, and *hoochee*, meaning patterned or painted. The angry torrent of water rushing by them indicated that it must have been storming all the way up the course of the sparkling stream to its source at Brasstown Bald, the highest jewel in the Appalachian chain draped around the neck of Georgia. With this much water pouring into the navigable part of the river below Columbus, it would be too dangerous to travel at night.

"We'd best extend our visit."

Lily's stomach churned as her mother voiced the words she had been dreading as she watched the swirling water. "But, but, Mama, if we don't go back with the *Wave* —well, you know Papa will be wanting you home. . . ."

"Yes, I know he will," Mrs. Edwards wavered. "I don't know." She shook her head. "Perhaps we should wait for the next boat."

"But that will be days," Lily wailed.

"The river won't look this bad to you a few miles downstream," Laurie's husband soothed his nervous sister-in-law.

"I guess you're right. And we should be getting home."

Lily sighed in relief.

After they were packed and ready, Cordelia Edwards regretted her decision. "It's just too dangerous on the river," she said with her double chin shaking. "We'd better take the stagecoach home."

"Now, Mama," Lily swallowed hard, "you know how the lurching of the stagecoach ride always sets off your rheumatism, and the trip takes so much longer. On the boat you can stay in bed, and the current will have us home in no time."

Mrs. Edwards finally agreed that the luxury of modern travel outweighed the danger. They bid Columbus farewell at noon on Monday.

Cordelia Edwards remained in her cabin shedding nervous tears, but Lily wrapped a cashmere shawl about her head and shoulders and went on deck to savor the excitement. A young man rode on the bow watching for snags and rocks and changes in the river. Lily leaned far over the rail and watched anxiously as they approached a bridge that had floated off its piers. The day before, the *Cardinal* had struck it. With a hole in her hull, she had gone to pieces and sunk, leaving both submerged and floating debris waiting to entrap the *Wave*.

As the ship's master, Harrison was constantly checking with Captain Allen, the mate, the pilot at the wheel, the striker pilot, and the engineer. There was no time for conversation, but Lily reveled in the vitality. Watching a point of interest, and feeling a warmth upon her, she turned to see Harrison's dark eyes smiling his approval of her sparkle.

At supper time, Lily ate hungrily of the lavish meal. She had repaired the wind damage to her hair and changed to her most becoming street toilet when the *Wave* reached the Eufaula wharf at seven o'clock.

A weary Harrison Wingate was on hand to speak to departing passengers. After he had taken Mrs. Edwards's hand and had been as gracious as possible, Lily extended her gloved fingers and spoke in a loud, firm voice.

"Thank you for a delightful voyage and for getting us here safely, Captain Wingate," she said pertly. Afraid to look at her mother, she continued in a voice that was far too loud, "We must repay you for your kindness. Won't you come and have supper with us tomorrow evening?"

Harrison hesitated, glancing at Mrs. Edwards who merely pursed her lips and said nothing. Seeing that she was not intending to add her invitation, he squeezed Lily's hand and replied, "Thank you very kindly, Miss Lily. I would be delighted."

Papa waved, and Mama was too absorbed with meeting him and securing their trunks to scold her.

Unfortunately, Green had returned from his business trip inland. That greatly complicated the situation. Lily pretended weariness and stayed in her room all of the next day to avoid both Mama and Green, but she could hardly contain her excitement concerning Harrison.

That evening she hovered nervously on the landing of the grand staircase, arranging and rearranging the flowers in the coffin niches to remain out of sight below stairs but be on hand to greet Harrison. Glimpsing him striding toward the house, she floated down the stairs with her face alight with joy.

"Wingate, old man, what a surprise to see you!" Green moved from the corner of the veranda where he had been smoking.

"Nice to see you again," replied Harrison cordially. "I hope you've found enough local planters willing to sell you their fall crop."

Lily joined the men and tried to chat lightly, but nervous tears filled her throat. She squeezed her eyes to slits and looked at them. These were not two schoolboys with whom she was flirting in an effort to keep both interested. Unsuspecting, the friends talked amiably. Seemingly they had no inkling that they were rivals.

Evidently, Mama had forgotten about her invitation to Harrison. Lily noticed out of the corner of her eye that when Mama was about to call them to supper she went back to have another place set.

Lily picked at her food. She took little part in the lively conversation that flowed from Green's adventures on the frontier to Harrison's travels on the river. She sighed thankfully when the meal was over and Papa reached for his box of cigars.

By prearrangement, Emma engaged Cordelia Edwards in conversation about a household problem as the ladies were excused. Lily slipped away.

Stationing herself in the back hall near the servants' entrance to the dining room, Lily unashamedly eavesdropped.

Harrison cleared his throat. "Mr. Edwards, there's a matter I would speak with you about quite seriously, sir."

"Yes? And what is that?" Mr. Edwards soft voice indicated that he was tired, satiated with food, and not ready for dilemmas.

"Well, sir, I realize that you do not know me—I'll be glad to provide information about my family background, sir. I. . ."

Lily strained forward, wondering what was happening in the uncomfortable silence. The cigar stench nearly made her retch.

"You see, sir, I love your daughter very much," Harrison blurted. "I have reason to believe that she returns my affection. I wish to ask you for her hand in marriage."

Something crashed to the floor.

"Sir, I am shocked!" Mr. Edwards's voice rose in power. "You have taken advantage of our hospitality. You presume—surely you haven't taken advantage of my daughter?"

"You insult *me*, sir!" Green shouted. "You betray our friendship even speaking the name of my intended bride!"

"Your intended? I didn't know. You told me you came here on business," Harrison stammered. "I'm sorry." His voice went limp. "You never mentioned her name. If I had known your intentions in the beginning, I would not have pressed my courtship, but now we are irrevocably in love."

Green growled angrily. "I had not rushed Miss Lily at her request." Green bit off each word with fury. "She said she was not ready for marriage but, I have been led to believe that as soon as she was ready, she would be mine."

"She has agreed to marry me, if you will give your permission, Mr. Edwards," Harrison said with quiet firmness. "I'm sorry my request has taken you by surprise."

Lily leaned her forehead against the doorjamb; misery gripped her.

"Well. . .you must give me time to think about this, to speak with Mrs. Edwards. . ."

"Surely you wouldn't consider . . ." Green shouted. Then he lowered his voice so that Lily, who was clinging to the wall, could barely hear. "You shall be hearing from me formally, sir. Through my second."

"Wait, friend." Harrison's voice had regained some of its usual calm strength. "We could not sully Miss Lily's name by anything so public as a duel."

"By no means," Green snarled, "but I say, sir, that I was cheated at cards on your steamer."

Harrison laughed offhandedly. "And you, sir, know that I warned you that gambler was a cheat, and you also know that the *Wave* bears a sign saying gentlemen who play cards for money, play at their own risk." His voice became placating. "I'm sorry if I offended you —"

"I say you are a liar. This affair is now in the hands of the seconds!"

"So be it," Harrison returned grimly. "Thank you for the hospitality of your table, Mr. Edwards. Good night."

Lily ran into the dark yard and stumbled around the house to meet Harrison as he left, hat in hand. Tears streamed down her cheeks. They walked across the yard stiffly apart, too miserable to speak or to touch each other. When they reached the gate he looked down at her sadly.

"I knew it would be bad," she sniffed, "but not this bad. I'm so sorry I couldn't prepare Papa, but I had no chance to see him without encountering Mama or Green."

His face blanched. "You should have told me about Green." Obviously feeling betrayed, he spoke gruffly, full of hurt.

"Oh, I should have, I should have, but I don't think of him at all when I'm with you," she wailed. "Believe me. I never cared for him. He doesn't love me. It was all Mama's plans. Papa knew I didn't want to marry him."

"But you let them think that you would."

The dead sound of his voice made her drop her face in her hands. He did nothing to comfort her weeping.

"I was wrong," she gulped, fighting for control. "I see it now. I thought only of myself." She tried to lean against him, but he stood back stiffly. "I have tried to tell them all, but I'm expected to do as I'm told. Oh, I was so afraid for a moment that Green might have a sword concealed in that cane of his. He might have killed you!"

"You are a child," he laughed sardonically. "Nowadays swords are used only in New Orleans—yes, he fancies New Orleans—but, the elite do not dive into the fray. The Code Duello is a highly ritualized affair that has only begun. I shall receive a written challenge delivered by his second." He sighed wearily.

"But you can't believe in dueling," she wailed. "For years sermons have been preached, laws have been passed. . . ."

"You know very well that all of the laws have carried no more enforcement than the sermons." Again he laughed in bitter irony. "Of course, I don't believe in dueling—but there's nothing that I can do. I must accept his challenge."

"If you left for awhile," she wailed. Even as she said it, she knew she could not bear his going.

"No!" He shook his head grimly. "He might resort to posting, naming me as a villain and a coward in an advertisement in the newspapers. I couldn't have your name . . ."

"I don't care about my name!" she cried out. "I only care about you!" She flung herself against his chest.

Stiffly, his arms closed around her. For a moment

he clung to her with longing; then, he stroked her hair gently and said as if speaking to a child, "Well-known men fight duels every day. Many of them are bloodless. Duels only become famous if they're fatal— Now scoot. Back in the house with you before your father comes after me, too." His laugh sounded false to both of them as he turned her around.

Her steps dragged as she trudged back to the house. The huge, white mansion was ablaze with light. It appeared that every candle in every chandelier and wall sconce was lit. There was no place to hide from her misery.

CHAPTER 7

LILY STEPPED INTO PANDEMONIUM. Mama had fainted. Screeching, Kitty ran about flapping her apron. Muttering ugly words, Green stamped down the black and white marble hall.

Lily clung to the doorjamb and waited until he had gone out the rear door. Her anxious fingers crumpled her handkerchief as her nerves were shredded.

Papa. Surely she could count on Papa to understand. He sat apart, sunk into his chair with both hands clapped over his bald head. Kneeling beside him, she patted his hand.

"Oh, Papa," she cried. "I should have prepared you, but you were gone all day, and I was afraid that—"

"You knew about this then?"

"Yes, Papa. I love Harrison. I want to be his wife."

"You're a child. Do you have any idea what kind of men run riverboats?" His voice croaked, then rose in indignation. "They are full of swaggering bravado.

They make a noisy exit from the wharf only to round the next bend and meet an ignominious end with everything they own crushed on a shoal of rock!"

"I know that steering a vessel through a twisting channel takes forthright determination," she said through clenched teeth. "But Harrison takes safety precautions and the gamble is worth the risk," she pleaded. "This modern world can't wait to move in a horse and wagon. I like being part of the excitement."

"It's out of the question!" Mama's angry voice made them jump. "No daughter of mine will marry a common riverboat gambler."

"He's not a gambler," Lily bristled.

"What would Laurie think!" Cordelia wailed and feigned another faint. Kitty ran in with smelling salts.

"Papa, Harrison is a fine, Christian man. The kind I want for my husband. I do not want to marry Green!"

"But we have let him think that you would," he answered resignedly. "His personal honor is at stake, and—"

"Surely, you don't condone dueling!" She bowed her head on his knee, then looked up at him with pleading eyes. "You must stop it!"

"Stronger men than I have tried to stop dueling ever since Burr killed Hamilton," he sighed wearily. "But when men in high office—even our presidents—feel they must live by this Code of Honor, what's to be done?"

"Much can be said in its favor." Mama's voice was sharp. Her moment of weakness had passed.

"Mama!" Lily exclaimed, shocked.

"The knowledge that a man will be called to account for false words or affronts to one's character—such as this social climber has made to you—are well guarded by the Code Duello." Cordelia Edwards's mouth was drawn down sternly and her double chins were firmly set. "Most girls your age would gladly risk the loss of a husband to have a hero in the family."

Lily tore at her hair. She turned pleading eyes to Papa who merely sat there rubbing his hand over his head.

"We will let Green take care of the intruder." Mrs. Edwards spoke with finality. "We shall not speak of it again!"

Lily fled in a storm of tears. In utter loneliness, she lay on her bed. Her wrenching sobs would subside momentarily only to freshen and wrack her again. When she could cry no more, she tiptoed down the hidden stairway and slipped out the doorway to the back porch.

The door to Green's room stood open. Silhouetted in the candlelight, he was cleaning a pair of wooden-handled, long-barreled pistols.

Hesitantly, she knocked, being careful not to further disgrace herself by stepping inside his room.

He looked up in surprise. With a glinty-eyed grimace, he came to the door and waved a gun under her nose. "These pistols were made in London by Wogdon. The balance is superb. Your honor will soon be avenged."

"No, Green, not for me—please." Weak and disheveled, she leaned against the porch wall.

"Your name won't enter in," he quickly assured her. "My challenge," he motioned toward the desk where pen and paper indicated that the note was already written, "merely names him a liar and a cheat."

"Oh, Green!" She fought a wave of nausea. "I'm sorry! I should have explained it to you first," she sighed heavily. "You were gone when I told him to come."

"You told him—you knew?" His sulky face bent close over hers. "You were promised to me."

"No. I never told you. I never said—"

"Not in words. But in actions."

She buried her face in her hands. "Yes, I admit it. It seemed as though we should make a perfect match—but—I can't help it. I fell in love with Harrison."

"You have insulted me." He drew himself up pompously. "I will forgive you if word never gets outside this house that you allowed him to ask for you."

But you would never let me forget it, Lily thought. Sadly, hopelessly, she climbed the stairs to her room. Foy. The thought flickered in her deadened brain. She dragged herself up to the belvedere.

He was there with his hurricane lamp. The fact that he was reading one of Sir Walter Scott's novels of chivalric derring-do made her know he was well aware that the gauntlet had been thrown down.

"One or both of them might be killed, you know," the owl-eyed little boy said matter-of-factly.

"Oh, Foy, I've begged them all. I can't stop the duel. Help me. Find out everything. Maybe I can stop them at the last minute."

"You know that can't be done, Sister," he replied as if he were the elder.

"I know. But I must be there."

The next day, she remained in bed, rising only to receive Foy's reports of the progress of the ritual.

Scratching lightly on Foy's bedroom door, Lily waited only a moment before he slipped out and joined her in the dark hallway. Grimacing, she knew he had slept little during the long night either. She had spent most of it on her knees claiming her Lord's promise to be with her through trials. Tired, yet seized with a frenzied excitement, she followed Foy down the hidden staircase. In the intense darkness before dawn, they felt their way to the stables and saddled their horses. Forcing themselves to walk slowly, they led the horses down the driveway past their parents' bedroom before they mounted.

"I don't know how I could have stood this without you, Foy," Lily said sorrowfully.

The boy said nothing, but slowly and purposefully he straightened his slumped shoulders and sat erect in his saddle.

The night had cooled little from the hundred degrees of the previous day. Lily's riding habit, soaked with perspiration, felt sticky in the humid darkness. In all of her eighteen years, she had never been so miserable.

Although word of the duel had only been whispered around Eufaula, Foy had easily learned of the appointed place, a secluded clearing on the banks of the Chattahoochee just across the county line. A ring of huge oak trees thickly hung with ghostly gray beards of Spanish moss sheltered the spot from prying eyes.

When Lily dismounted, her knees buckled. With her face as gray as her pearly riding habit, she tethered Prince who was lathered with salty sweat. Summoning all of her strength, she crept to a spot behind a thick-trunked oak where she could peer out without being seen. Draped on the spreading branches, shrouds of Spanish moss shivered as they breathed the life-giving, humid air. Of matching color with the hair-like plant, Lily blended in a blur, swaying as it swayed.

Flat on his stomach, Foy slithered closer.

A group of men had already assembled. Moving about on springing feet, Green stood out from the rest in his slim, doeskin trousers and white, ruffled shirt.

Harrison arrived. Lily's heart lurched at the sight of his sagging face. Would he ever forgive her for putting him in this awful position? Teardrops rolled unnoticed down her cheeks. Idly, she wondered why he wore such a large, ill-fitting coat in this heat. The two participants stood apart from the rest at the far ends of the clearing.

Captain Allen went forward as his second to inspect the flintlock pistols. He carried the leather case to Wingate who deliberated, then lifted one of the pistols that had a barrel fully fifteen inches long. Evidently Green was granting a trial shot. Allen placed a small paper on a tree. Harrison raised the heavy pistol heavenward then slowly, deliberately aimed and fired.

"Whew!" Foy whistled. He scrambled back to Lily. "He's a crack shot! Maybe we don't have to worry."

Lily gritted her teeth, knowing that speed counted as much as accuracy. Harrison was Foy's unquestioned champion, but a sudden surge of affection for her cousin, heightened by the knowledge that she had wronged him, made her realize that she did not want his blood spilt either.

Clenching both fists over her mouth to keep herself from screaming, Lily watched the ritual proceed with excruciating precision. The seconds flipped a coin high in the air. Green won the toss. He fixed positions. Lily bit her fist savagely when Harrison moved as directed until his black coat was silhouetted sharply against the crimson streaks of dawn as the sun rose behind the Chattahoochee and turned it red as blood. Silently the adversaries met back to back.

"One, two," the giver of the word counted slowly, "three, four." With guns down at their sides, they paced stiffly. "Five, six, seven, eight, nine, ten. Fire!"

Blat!

The short, harsh sound echoed and re-echoed through the forest. Eyes shut, Lily swayed. Slowly she realized there had been only one shot. She opened her eyes. Acrid smoke curled from Green's pistol. She jerked toward Harrison. He still stood. Unflinching, he held his gun down at his side.

Green stared at him, recoiled.

"Back to the mark, sir!" cried the man who was giver of the word.

Green folded his arms. Head up, he stood defiantly, waiting.

Harrison raised his gun slowly, deliberately. Aimed. There was a hollow "clock" as the hammer stopped at half-cock. Swiftly, he lifted it over his head and fired into the air. Lily sank to the ground.

Green was angry, still demanding satisfaction. She knew that the Code Duello allowed three, but no more encounters. Lying prostrate on the damp ground, Lily felt she could not bear it again. The men returned to opposite sides, and the seconds marched forward.

Green's second shouted his message, "Turn and shoot. Providence will favor truth and right with victory."

Allen spoke quietly, but in ringing tones, "Captain Wingate has no desire to harm you. You are entitled to kill him, but he wronged you unknowingly. He does not want your blood on his hands, nor his on yours. He will shoot the sky."

Lily could not breathe as the terrible pacing off began again.

"Gentlemen are you ready?"

"Ready," replied Green.

"Yes, sir," said Harrison.

"Fire!"

Blat!

One shot. Lily blinked. Harrison had fired quickly upward. Green snarled, shot quickly. Harrison's gun dropped. Blood spurted from his arm. Blood was spilt. Green had satisfaction. It was over. Lily retched violently.

The attending surgeon rushed to Harrison's side. Lily longed to run to him, but she dared not be seen. She silently pressed her initialed handkerchief into Foy's hand. The child's crumpled face twitched back tears. He skittered after Harrison who was departing into the mossy mists of morning. Stiffening in surprise, he took the token, turned, looked back, but could not see her.

Glumly, brother and sister remounted and headed toward Barbour Hall. Halfway home, they dismounted, wept in each other's arms, then finished the ride in silence. With day fully broken, their disappearance had been discovered. Furious, Mama forbade them to leave the grounds until further notice.

Emma came to Lily's bedside, bathed her face with cold cloths, and coaxed her to sip a cooling drink. She reported that Green had exiled himself to New

Orleans for a decent interval, but she could secure no word of Harrison.

As soon as Lily recovered somewhat, she thought of Foy and how disappointed he must be in his champion. He might even think Harrison a coward for not fighting more conventionally.

Weakly she climbed to the belvedere where Foy sat in kingly exile pouring over his books.

"Foy, I'm sorry. Were you terribly disappointed in Captain Wingate?"

He surprised her by grinning happily. "I was at first. I wanted him to kill that Green," he said emphatically. "But," he nodded sagely, "that would have been wrong. After I thought about it, I realized that what he did took a lot more courage."

She nodded solemnly.

"And Green—for all his talk of honor—broke his own code."

Lily's eyebrows lifted quizzically.

"Yes. You see, it frequently happens that an honorable man who accepts a challenge will fire into the air." He paused, proud of his superior knowledge. "It is then held scandalous for the other party to fire again."

"Well!" she exclaimed. "But, I guess Green just couldn't be satisfied without drawing blood. Oh, Foy, I've just got to know how Captain Wingate is. I must see him!"

"I'll slip out when Mama takes her nap."

"You'll risk a thrashing!"

Foy shrugged.

Harrison's scowl and the grim set of his lips as he moved uncertainly from behind the stables and walked across the back garden made Lily retreat behind a pink fountain of crepe myrtle blossoms and shut her eyes to steady herself. Taking a deep breath, she shyly stepped into view. The air between them shimmered with rising waves of heat, blurring her tearful vision.

A smile lifted his whole body. He caught his breath as he had the first time he saw her. Needing nothing more, she ran to meet him, unmindful of her wildly tilting hoop.

At his side she stopped, suddenly feeling unmaidenly. "Oh, Harrison, you looked so angry with me just now."

"What?" He reached out tentatively to touch her shoulder. "Oh, I just felt awkward—I don't like deception, but Foy said to meet you back by the ha-ha wall."

"I'm sorry." She bowed her head. Shyness overwhelmed her again. "My family was so awful to you. I'm sorry." Gingerly she stretched out one finger to the sling on his right arm. "Is it bad?"

"A mere nick," he shrugged, and then had to hide the flicker of pain the gesture gave him.

"You shouldn't have gone." His voice was gruff with emotion. "I was afraid you wouldn't want to see me again."

"Why?" she exclaimed, incredulous.

"I'm sure I didn't fulfill your daydreams of a knight in shining armor. And Foy. I know I disillusioned him."

"Huh," she snorted, "couldn't you look at the sparkle in his eyes and know he thought you're the bravest man he's ever seen?"

He smiled. "And you?"

She cocked her head to one side saucily. "I'm not sure whether I think you're brave or foolhardy. How could you risk your life just standing there taking his first fire?"

"Well," he grinned sheepishly, "I did take the precaution of wearing an ill-fitting coat—hoping he'd misjudge the position of my heart."

"Oh, my dearest darling, he might have killed you." Lily melted against him burying her face on his chest as the restraint between them dissolved.

Harrison's strong left arm tightened around her. He kissed the top of her dark curls. She lifted her face to him with eyes full of love and stood on tiptoe to meet his tender kiss.

Too filled with emotion to speak further, they silently strolled along the path by the ha-ha wall.

Harrison broke the silence at last. "I understand Green is gone."

"Yes," she murmured from deep within a dream. Rousing herself, she added, "Foy says he broke his own precious ritual by shooting you after you had fired into the air."

"Yes. That went against the code." He stopped and looked down at her and said earnestly, "But, you must understand, I impugned his honor. He belongs to a dueling society. He wanted to draw blood, but he's not as bad as you think." He seemed to want to clear his friend. "He purposely winged me. If he had wanted to, he could have killed me easily. His Code Duello means everything to—"

Lily shuddered. "I'm glad you live by a higher code," she said simply.

Harrison chuckled. "It's one not easy to follow. I wanted to shoot him, sweep you into my arms, and carry you away," he admitted ruefully. "I struggled all night. Loving one's enemy is not impossible, but turning your cheek from an insult—I'd never realized how difficult that is. But I kept on hearing a quiet voice in my head saying, 'Turn the other cheek,'" he laughed self-consciously. "It's hard. Green's insults are still ringing in my ears. But I'll survive that," he shrugged. "I couldn't let him make me a murderer."

"I'm afraid I'll never be as completely submissive to the lordship of Christ as you are."

Embarrassed at her praise, he changed the subject. "What do we do now? Is there any chance that your parents will accept me after this?"

"Oh, there must be, there must be," she cried. "I'll speak to them at supper. Can you meet me back here at dusk?"

Sadly, they parted, knowing that the next few hours would stretch interminably between them.

Unable to eat a bite, Lily pled her love for Harrison.

"It is totally out of the question!" Cordelia Edwards banged her fork vehemently. "You have behaved like a spoiled child, and I will tolerate no more insolence. You will do exactly—"

"We will not discuss it further," Papa said firmly, surprising them both as he stepped into control of the conversation. "Lily, you promised you would not do as my cousin Lucinda did."

"No, Papa," she bowed her dark head. "I won't break with you and Mama. I won't run away and marry without your blessing."

Harrison found her at the back of the garden crying. He lifted her chin and made her smile up at him. He dropped his lips to hers lightly, tenderly. "Is there no hope?"

She drew a long, shuddering sigh and shook her head.

He stroked her dark, disheveled curls away from her face. "They don't even know me. We rushed them too much! If only we had more time, but I must go away." His usually smiling face sagged with a pain that matched her own.

"Oh, no!" She sank weakly into the curve of his sheltering arm.

"It's best for now. Was your father's answer an absolute refusal?"

"Mama's was, but Papa—maybe he will be more open," she mumbled. She lifted her head from his shoulder and looked into his eyes. "Oh, Harrison, you do understand?" she pleaded. "I love you and I want to be your wife, but I cannot flagrantly disobey my parents. It wouldn't be right just to run away and marry." Her soulful eyes beseeched him.

"Yes," he answered quietly. "It hurts, but I do understand." He drew himself up with a dignity that built a wall between them.

"Oh, Harrison, love me, love me. There must be a way," she wailed. "Give me time," she begged stroking his smooth, tanned cheek. "They will change. They must change!"

"I'll wait for you my darling, but each day will be an eternity." He kissed her tear-streaked face.

Silently, hand in hand, they paced the back of the garden. The beautiful view was unbroken as they gazed sadly across the meadow. It looked as if they could walk on forever; nevertheless, they had come to the end of Lily's domain. Even though the view was unspoiled, the ha-ha wall was at their feet. Built down in a ditch so that it was unseen, the wall kept domestic animals, that roamed loose, out of the flower garden.

Harrison took both her hands and pressed kisses upon them. "Please write to me."

"Oh, I will. And you write. In my name. I won't deceive them any more."

"I must go now. We're scheduled to sail at daylight. You'll come?"

"I can't. But I'll be watching."

He kissed her tenderly, pouring out his heart's longing. The darkness closed around them, and for a moment they existed in the world alone. She breathed a shuddering sigh, and the heavy perfume of the tea olive made the bitter-sweetness of her love almost too much to bear.

Sunlight, turning the belvedere windows into diamonds, dazzled her swollen eyes. Lily knew that the height made Emma dizzy, but it helped a great deal to have her friend standing with her. Tears streamed down Emma's pale cheeks as she shared Lily's heartbreak and relived her own.

Uhmmmm! Uhmmmm! It had never sounded so mournful. Black smoke, floating above the treetops, drifted down the Chattahoochee.

"Oh, Emma, that graveyard of a river is between us again. Please, God, don't let it be forever." She dropped her head on Emma's shoulder and sobbed.

CHAPTER 8

FRUSTRATED, LILY PACED the garden throughout the lonely days that followed. She would walk as far as the ha-ha wall and stand gazing sadly into the meadow where the cattle and deer roamed wild and free. This unseen barrier was an illusion. It appeared that the garden was without the usual fence to keep out the cattle that foraged at will; however, Lily knew that only her level gaze could continue into openness. Below her feet, a wide ditch had been dug. Wild things could wander in and out of the ditch, but a solid wall, erected against the garden side, defeated them from tasting the flowers.

A bitter sensation rising in her throat made her give up her walks and return to her old haunt above the treetops in the belvedere. There she could see the course of the river punctuated by white puffs from the steamboats plying its muddy waters. With her body rigid, she stood on the widow's walk, but her spirit floated away on a raft of daydreams.

Mama and Papa eyed her warily. Whenever she walked into the room, their bodies stiffened with tension, their hands dropped straight to their sides, and their darting eyes stated plainly that there was no way to bridge the gap.

With their demeanor totally isolating her, she was sustained only by her daily vigil for a letter. At last it came. Feeling alive again, she ran up the six flights of stairs to the privacy of the belvedere before she opened the message from her sweetheart. Kissing the signature, she closed her eyes and imagined him sitting in his cabin on the lofty hurricane deck, smiling with a crinkle around his eyes as he thought of her. Her finger traced his words and, love warmed, stroked her cheek as she read.

July 19, 1858

Along the Chattahoochee

Darling Lily,

I write this hoping I may be able to send it sometime this week by a vessel sailing your way as I so greatly wish that I could be. My receiving your letters will be uncertain, but please write to me. I will be in the city of Columbia, Alabama, for several days and in Apalachicola, Florida, for as much as a week.

I am terribly lonesome for you. I will not ask you to go against your parents for I know that would not follow your principles. I love the beauty of your character and soul even more than the loveliness of your face, which always floats before me. Please send me a picture so that I may feel I am touching you.

What can I do to plead my case with your mother? No one could ever take better care of you than I. I love you so much and long for the day that I can call you my wife.

The gentleman who is to carry this letter has just come up and says he must go immediately. Give my love to Emma.

God bless you.

I love you dearly.

Harrison H. Wingate

Reading and rereading his letter, Lily realized that Harrison did not understand the reason for her parents' refusal of their marriage. For this much she was glad. Throughout the day as she carried the letter about with her, touching it to feel Harrison near, she felt happy and warm. Even though the question of his social class had no solution, she was not of the temperament to give up and spend her time weeping hopelessly. Before she went to bed that night, she kissed the letter again and carefully placed it beneath her pillow. In the morning she read the letter again. Then she surreptitiously lifted the pin that secured the secret drawer in the rosewood lap desk and lovingly placed the letter inside.

Lily eagerly waited for an opportunity to go to the daguerreian gallery to have a likeness taken. At last her chance to go downtown came when Emma had to visit the dentist to have a tooth filled. Remembering the most approving light in Harrison's eyes had been when when she wore the white organdy with its frothy ruffles, she donned that frock and arranged her hair in soft curls. After sitting six times before the big box camera, she got a pleasing likeness. The stiff daguerreotype, on silver plate, showed the fine details of her dress and the printing on the little hymnbook she held in her hand. She could hardly wait to send the picture and the book to Harrison.

Several days later while the girls were shopping, they heard that Julian McKenzie would be leaving on the *Laura* the next morning. Excitedly, Lily hurried home because she knew that she could send her letter and package by him. Tilting her head for a moment of thought, she began to pour out her heart.

July 30, 1858

Eufaula, Alabama

I expect, Captain Wingate, that you have concluded ere this that I do not intend writing. I heard in town that the *Laura* will be leaving tomorrow and I could at last find opportunity to send you the likeness and my love.

My heart aches that I was such a thoughtless child to allow you to walk into the lion's den unprepared. I should have managed some way to tell Papa. I suppose I expected them to capitulate immediately, seeing that my happiness is at stake. Perhaps I am growing up a little, for after many tears, I am beginning to understand that they think they have my best interest at heart.

Alas! I know not how to change their minds.

You are constantly in my thoughts. So strongly do I imagine myself beside you on the boat that I can almost feel the wind in my hair. I envy you the excitement. My days are quiet. I attend prayer meeting and church services, make social calls in the afternoon, and take long walks. I go frequently to the graveyard beside the little stream that winds its way below our house. Tis a lovely, quiet retreat. It offers peace and solitude and seems to fit my mood. While there, I am engaged in reading *Grace Truman* with much interest.

At night, I vie with Foy for the use of the belvedere. There I pray for you. May the Lord keep you safe from the dangers which beset you. My dearest friend, we must also pray that God will make a way for us to become man and wife.

Goodbye.

Yours, Lily

Lily's spirits rose as she sent the tangible evidence of her love on its way. She was singing, "O Happy Day That Fixed My Choice," when she re-entered Barbour Hall. Seated in the parlor, Mr. and Mrs. Edwards looked up in surprise at her sudden merriment.

Snatching at the chance, Lily greeted them, "Good afternoon, Papa, Mama," she nodded politely. "Please, may I speak with you?" Her mother started to shake her head, but Lily hurried on, "I know that you want the best for me, and I appreciate the wisdom of your advice." Her voice trembled. "But I'm old enough now to know what I want to do with my life."

Cordelia Edwards was taking in breath, swelling with indignation. Her husband surprised her by speaking first.

"Marriage is too important to be entrusted to youth, Lily dear," Clare Edwards said gently. "You have been carried away by love and passion just as surely as young Foy has by this dashing figure who seems to lead such an exciting life, but—"

"Matrimony is the royal road to wealth and social advancement," her mother interrupted. "Such essential matters must be left with the parents. We will discuss it no more."

"But, Mama. . ."

"Don't talk back to me."

Lily swallowed, trying desperately to hold a shred of adulthood, but tears seemed to be rising from her toes and filling her whole body.

Haughtily, Mrs. Edwards stood too quickly. Groaning, she clutched her back but continued speaking firmly. "The minute Green returns, we will announce your engagement to him. We must move quickly to arrest any breath of scandal. We cannot have anyone whispering about your indiscreet behavior!"

Stunned, Lily stared at one then the other; they presented an unrelenting wall. She fled in a storm of tears.

Lily spent many hours sobbing on her bed. Pale and listless, she moved through the ensuing days not knowing or caring what she did. She existed only for another letter. When she received one, her joy turned to sorrow at Harrison's deep hurting, and her eyes were shining with tears as she read.

July 29, 1858

Columbia, Alabama

My Sweet Lily,

Another vessel in today and no letter for me. Why have you not written? I am blue, very blue indeed, afraid you might have changed your mind. Do you wish to obey your parents and forget me? I believed you when you said you truly loved me. Oh, how I hope it is merely lack of mail arrangements. Send letters to McKenzie or Atkins & Durrham to be forwarded whenever vessels leave. Numerous vessels have arrived and not one word for me.

I wish that you could see Columbia with me. As the boat docks, the passengers are called to the steamer deck to see the "chocolate layer cake," a huge rock that so resembles one. The rock marks the port of Columbia. It is a hub of the wiregrass section. People coming to Columbia for freight and supplies are provided with a camping enclosure for their wagons and livestock. Many sleep in the covered wagons while waiting for their shipments. It is a scene of much activity and excitement that you would enjoy very much.

Do I fool myself in thinking that you would? I know you have been raised a lady, sheltered from the common people. Did I take advantage of your youth and the romance of the moonlight upon the water to dare to kiss you and dream you could be mine?

You will break my heart if you say this is so, but knowing would be better than wondering.

Please write soon.

I love you dearly.

H.H.W.

Frantic at his words and her inability to communicate with him, Lily enlisted the aid of Foy. Daily she had lessened fighting with him and chasing him when he shot Chinaberries at her with a pop gun made from a hollowed elder branch. Now she saw him daily as her only ally. The boy had more freedom than she to roam the riverfront. He gladly agreed to take a letter for her and thought he could manage to get it off immediately.

August 10, 1858

Eufaula, Alabama

My heart breaks, Captain Wingate, that you doubt me. Surely you know my love for you is true and everlasting! I long to share your life. How I would enjoy meeting people from different environments and learning more about this world and God's creatures.

I hope by now you have received my letters and are recovered from the "blues." You might have known that I had written. Did I not promise to do so? I will write you every week, but right now there are only two boats running regularly between here and Apalachicola, and very often I do not know when they are here. Brother Foy has come to my aid in getting letters off to you as he admires you more than any man he has ever seen.

Mama is suffering from rheumatism. Papa sent to Hamilton, Georgia, to a physician there, for some medicine that cured a lady worse off than Mama. I do hope that it may have some good effect on her for I hate to cross her with her suffering so.

Good night.

Yours,

Lily

As she reread the letter and added kisses to the signature, she could imagine her mother's reaction if she should intercept their love letters. Although she was not hiding the fact that she was corresponding with Captain Wingate, she knew that her parents would continue to disapprove of him merely because he possessed no wealth or prominence. A person's family name meant everything to Mama.

The temperature was already in the eighties soon after the sun rose. Emma had not tried to comfort Lily during her restless night. Now she looked at her with compassion in her soft, blue eyes.

"Let's slip out before anyone sees us and take a walk," whispered Emma. "This day is really going to steam."

"Yes, I'd like to get away," Lily sighed. She pushed up her long hair that was already wet against her neck and caught it in a silken net. "It's so hot. Don't you think I could leave off one petticoat?"

"No." Emma responded quickly. "If your mother thought I wasn't making you behave like a lady—

Lily, the only joy in my life comes from being with you."

Sighing, Lily agreed. Hats in hand, they tiptoed out of the house. They walked in silence as they followed the winding stream until they reached the seclusion of the family graveyard.

"Oh, Emma, what must I do? I love my parents. I respect their advice. I don't want to rush into the wrong thing." She took off her hat and fanned at a pesky swarm of gnats. The heat-heightened colors and scents of the wildflowers and buzzing of the insects seemed to press in upon her.

"I don't know how to advise you," Emma replied. "I only know that my grandfather never relented." She bowed her blonde head sadly. Holding onto the cold, marble shaft of a monument, she continued so softly that Lily had to lean toward her to hear. "You can see for yourself what became of my life."

"I don't believe Mama and Papa will ever give their permission either." Lily's voice was flat, devoid of hope. "I promised Papa I would not break with them and marry without their blessing." She had cried until there were no more tears. She felt dry to her soul.

They wandered through the graveyard and back to the stream. Lily cleared a spot on the bank and sat down with her skirt mushrooming around her. The little creek was nearly dry, and Lily had to reach far down to cool her fingers in the sparkling water which bubbled from a nearby spring.

"It's thrilling to be loved by a man who faces his life with so much strength and courage. I enjoy being cherished." Her face was pale and she lifted tortured eyes to Emma. "Do you think I could learn to fit into his world?"

"I don't know," she shook her head. Emma was too afraid of snakes to go near the refreshing water. She stood leaning against the rough bark of a tall pine. Her expression showed concern. "I wish I could advise you, but it really depends on what kind of person you are deep down."

Lily's lower lip trembled. "Knowing my parents won't agree, do you think that if I really love him enough to put him first. . ." She swallowed hard, almost unable to voice the words. "Does it mean I should set him free?"

Emma picked up a rock and threw it into the water. "That was the choice I made," she said bitterly.

"But wasn't your case a little different?" Lily lifted quizzical eyebrows. "For love to last in a marriage, it should be based on both partners' love of God."

"That's true, but if I hadn't been forbidden to see him, might I not have led him to accept Jesus as his personal Savior?"

"Possibly, but important changes in a person's life should come before a marriage commitment is made. I believe God ordained marriage as a permanent basis for building a Christian home. Oh Emma," she wrung her wet fingers, "as hard as it was, you could not go back on your faith in Christ or your duty to your family. But I can't see what I should do. What changes must I make within myself?"

As they trudged back home, the still August air lay heavily upon them. Red dust from the road plastered their sticky skin. Kitty had been sent to find them and summon them to Mama's bedside. Lily spoke to her crossly. The long-limbed girl's ebony face drooped with hurt because Lily was usually kind. Lily hurried obediently to do her mother's bidding.

The three presented themselves meekly at the huge master bedroom at the rear of the second floor. Cordelia Edwards lay in a massive bed with straight walnut posts lifting a high, throne-like canopy. All the shutters were swung over the windows, and the girls strained to adjust their eyes to the shadowy room.

Gasping with pain and clutching her neck and back as she tried to sit up among the many pillows, Mrs. Edwards told the girls they would have to take over her duties until the spell of acute rheumatism subsided. She instructed Emma in handling the servants and gave her the set of keys. She did not relinquish this emblem of her domain lightly. Normally, Cordelia Edwards rose from her bed long before any of her servants and rested only on the Sabbath.

Looking then to Lily, she said, "You must make a condolence call for me. Mrs. Pugh has lost a lovely babe, the fourth or fifth she has buried."

"Yes ma'am," Lily replied and turned immediately to do her bidding, Her mother was a good woman who was always on hand whenever a need arose in the community.

"And, oh yes," Mrs. Edwards called after her, "stop by Mrs. Morrison's house. I heard this morning of her extreme illness. She has long been suffering from consumption."

As Lily proceeded toward her sad errands, she foresaw her mother as an invalid who would constantly need her. She would expect Lily to carry out the Christian service she had begun. Lily well knew that girls in her station were always expected to sacrifice their happiness cheerfully if their parents needed them at home. Sighing, she also knew that the blessing to marry Harrison would never come. Squaring her shoulders, she resigned herself to the life of a spinster, remaining in her mother's house, for she would not marry Green. She would have to stay at home; she must write and tell Harrison. This was the only course open to her. She loved Harrison so much that she must put his welfare first. It would not be fair to keep him hoping. He could find someone else. She had no choice but to write Harrison and set him free.

First, she must do her mother's bidding. After freshening her appearance, she started down the street with Kitty in attendance. Arriving at the Morrison house first, she stood trembling in the circle of friends assembled around the bed. She did not feel prepared to be with this group of older ladies watching Mrs. Morrison's struggles with death. The woman spoke weakly but firmly to them of the great importance of a preparation for death and her perfect willingness to go to God. As she breathed out her life sweetly, Lily left the room sobbing. Released by what she had witnessed, her tears flowed for her own life. It seemed equally at an end.

Feeling that she could stand no more but doggedly determined to do as she was told, she continued to the two-story clapboard home on Randolph Avenue built by United States Senator James L. Pugh. The pall of death was thrown over this home also. Clammy and miserable, Lily walked across the wide porch.

As she started across the entrance hall, a child about eighteen months old toddled toward her. With dancing blue eyes and a smile that spread her plump cheeks, she lifted tiny arms to Lily. Scooping her up spontaneously, Lily was welcomed with a huge hug. She kissed the adorable curls and handed the child a brown-eyed Susan she had idly plucked.

"Thank coo," her tiny voice crooned. She struggled free of Lily's arms and started away in an uncertain, tottering step that made Lily want to help her. "Ma-ma," she excitedly called, "Ma-ma. Flower."

Lily followed her into the twin parlors. Not knowing what to say to the grieving mother, she hoped her presence expressed her sympathy. Even though this visit was also sad, the vibrant joy of this surviving child entranced Lily. She left smiling, but the smile faded as she realized that the only way she would have children to love would be teaching a Sunday school class as Emma did. Emma's life was over. Now, her life was over, too.

Her spirits sank further as she returned past the Morrison house. She would have to go back later to help write the funeral invitations and affix the black ribbons so that they could be hand-carried to friends on surrounding plantations. For now, she must report back to her mother.

Released at last, she went to her room and sat at her desk gritting her teeth. She must write before she lost her resolve to put Harrison's welfare ahead of the happiness she gained from simply knowing he loved her.

Tears splattered the paper as she told Harrison that she would not marry him. She pressed her hands to her temples and pulled at her hair making it stand out wildly. Ink smeared her cheeks as she wrestled with the longings of her heart. At last she wrote firmly that she released him from any promises to her. Sealing the letter, she went in search of Foy.

The small boy looked at her with his mouth gaping foolishly and waited for a second command before he replied, "Yes, there's a steamer due in today. I was on my way to the wharf now."

Lily gulped back tears and nodded wordlessly as she handed him the letter. She turned and fled up the stairs to the seclusion of the belvedere. Just as she climbed through to the top, she saw a carriage arriving.

Out stepped Green Bethune.

CHAPTER 9

"OH, NO, NOT NOW," she wailed aloud. Hoping he had not looked up and seen her, she scurried down the narrow passageway to her room. Her image in the looking glass surprised her. Tear streaks made roads on her face through valleys of attic dust and ink. She washed thoroughly at her lavatory. By the time she had brushed her hair, Emma arrived to say the family was assembled and summoning her.

Sedately, she descended the stairs and extended her hand to Green. Averting her eyes from his, she looked toward the parlor and blinked in surprise. Three wooden barrels were set undecorously in the middle of the room. Their tops had been removed, and straw was spilling everywhere.

"Lily-honey, I've brought you some wedding gifts from New Orleans," Green spoke exuberantly, his bearded face beaming.

"My goodness,' she breathed, moving mechanically to steady herself against the white marble fireplace. The huge Belgian mirror reflected a scene of gaiety, as Mama and Papa opened their presents. Lily traced her finger over the sévres vase and tried to grasp the situation. The flattery her parents were pouring as oil upon Green's head and his responsive laughter spoke clearly to Lily. Her life had been decided for her. They had all dismissed her love for Harrison as a young girl's folly.

Emma stood apart from the group. *Harrison would have brought her a present, too,*Lily thought. Knowing she must forget him, she allowed Green to lead her to the small Chippendale settee where he sat close beside her and handed her one package after another. Numb, feeling that she viewed the scene without really being there, she pressed her spine against the carved mahogany leaves and scrolls of the back and gritted her teeth. She opened endless gifts and tried valiantly to show proper appreciation.

Streaks of rose washed over the Georgian silver fruit basket she held in her lap. Lily gazed sadly out of the tall windows. The day had spent itself along with her tears. Her dreams had died. Suddenly her girlhood seemed over. Daydreams must give way to practicality. She felt unbelievably old.

Dinner was announced. The glittering prisms of the chandeliers made her tired eyes ache. The chicken and dumplings did not appeal to her. Green ate voraciously of the heavy, greasy food and talked excitedly of his western tour. He spoke in the sweeping, positive statements of one accustomed to being told he was right and granted every whim.

Suddenly she realized that everyone was looking at her expectantly, waiting for her to reply. "Wha—what did you say?"

"I said," Green repeated, "that I found New Orleans enchanting. It would be a perfect place to begin our honeymoon."

"But, I . . ." Lily began. She must put a stop to this, must tell them she preferred not to marry at all.

"New Orleans is especially lovely in the spring," Cordelia Edwards interrupted. All of the ravages of her pain were either vanished or well masked since Green's sudden appearance. "Lily, an early spring wedding would be beautiful. We could far outshine Betty Flournoy's."

"But, Mama. . . ."

Foy ambled in at that moment mumbling an apology for being late. He had gone to the waterfront to take her letter, Lily realized miserably. Her refusal to marry Harrison would soon be in his hands. Foy's hair seemed to bristle as he glared at her.

Green ignored the boy and continued to talk about New Orleans. "You'll like the old French Quarter or Vieux Carre. The dwellings are patterned after the houses of southern France, Spain, and Italy. Heavy doors, directly on the flagstone streets, open into the most delightful courtyards. He took another steaming biscuit and spread it with butter. "I'll take you to an old restaurant, Antoine's, for Pompano Pontchartrain."

No one was allowing Lily to say a word. It seemed no one cared what she thought. Her liquid brown eyes sought Emma's, but her friend would not look at her. As Emma left the table to whisk the cream for dessert, Lily reflected upon the sadness of Emma's existence. The spinster's place was a lonely plane too far above the servants for friendship, too far below the family for inclusion. The sweet girl had so much love to give;

yet, there was no way for her to escape or do anything else with her life.

The pecan pie, piled high with whipped cream, was far too rich and Lily feared nausea would overwhelm her. As soon after the meal as politely possible she pled a headache and escaped to the solitude of her room.

Throughout the night, Lily tossed and turned in the soft feather bed and rehearsed the words she would say to Green in the morning. She planned to tell him firmly that she would not marry him. If she could not marry her true love, she would remain a spinster. Dawn streaked the sky before she slept.

When she washed her face in her lavatory the next morning, she noticed that her eyes were red and swollen. No matter, she sighed. Green never looked into them as Harrison did. Dressing without much care, she went quietly into the hallway.

Creak! A wide floorboard gave her away. Mama looked out from the sitting room at the front of the hall. She used it as her morning room to go over her budget and the ceaseless stream of household activities that accompanied providing for her family and servants.

"Come here, Lily," she called, "I'm making lists for a party to announce your engagement."

"Mama, I'd planned to talk with Green this morning, and . . . " she hesitated. Mama's attention was focused on her lists that scattered over the light beechwood writing table of her secretary. Lily stepped across the room and opened the shutters to the balcony hoping the draft of fresh air would clear her aching head.

Down below, Green waited. Seeing her, he bowed

slightly, tipped his silk hat, and waved it excitedly. "I have the runabout ready." He called. "I want to show you something."

"Green's waiting, Mama," Lily said. The moment she had dreaded all night had come.

"You young people run along," Mrs. Edwards's chins shook as she smiled and nodded. "I'll tell you my plans later."

Lifting her skirt to free her feet, Lily ran down the stairs before her mother could send a chaperone. Surely with their engagement pending, they could be seen alone. She would risk the scandal because she knew a man with Green's pride must be confronted without someone listening.

A lazy smile spread over his perfect features at her apparent enthusiasm. Green helped her into the small buggy with a flourish and headed the horse up College Hill.

"I hope you slept well and are feeling better this morning." Green's pale blue eyes roamed over her with the approval of possession. Without waiting for a reply to this customary, polite greeting, he plunged into his plans, "I wanted to show you a choice of building sites."

"Green, I just really don't know how to. . ." She shifted uncomfortably against the red leather seat that was so narrow that it pressed her too closely against him. All of her planned phrases of the night had flown from her brain.

"Now, now, you just sit back and relax. We'll look at several places, but you don't have to decide today." He patted her hand soothingly. Looking quickly around and seeing no one, he brushed a bristly kiss across her cheek.

The clop-clop-clop of the horse's hooves thudded in Lily's aching head. She could think of nothing to say The creaking of the buggy scraped like fingernails against her brain.

"Whoa!" Green commanded and pulled the horse to a stop near the top of the hill. "I thought you might like this place. Since your mother isn't well, it would be convenient for you to visit her from here."

Lily looked into his handsome face. He was making every effort to be charming. "That's thoughtful of you," she murmured.

"James Kendall is seasoning wood to build up here," he gestured. "I understand he is planning an Italianate design. You might like that also. The tall erect form is majestic on the crest of a hill, and belvederes or even small cupolas afford a view of the Chattahoochee and the green hills beyond. . . ."

Lily shivered in spite of the August heat. "Green, you must listen to me. I could never look out across the river without thinking of Harrison."

A scowl creased Green's brow and his bearded cheeks contorted as he clenched his jaw. With obvious effort, he controlled his temper. After a long pause, he said between his teeth, "I'm willing to forget our meddlesome friend." Then he continued in a surprisingly even tone, "When I was seventeen, I thought I was in love with someone beneath me, too. Perhaps it's merely guilt because we have so much more than they. I guess it's part of growing up—having a hopeless, bitter-sweet first love."

"But, Green . . ." she protested. She grasped his arm trying to force him to listen, but he was smiling fondly as if she were a two year old.

"You were such a child when I first came. But I've

waited patiently for you to grow up. You're much more mature now." His patronizing tone changed to harshness. "We'll never speak of Wingate again—unless we hear of a boiler bursting and the gallant captain going down with his ship." The rumble of his laughter held an unmistakable sound of menace.

Clutching the ivory handle of her parasol until her knuckles turned white, Lily bit her lip miserably. She felt hot and sticky. All of the curls so carefully crimped into her hair with an iron heated in the fireplace were becoming lank in the humidity. Her combs were slipping and hair was sliding down her neck. She wondered why he was determined to appear forgiving.

Heading the horse down the hill, Green answered her thought, "I left South Carolina with my family's blessing for marrying you. With the blending of our fortunes and our blood, we can build an empire."

At that moment the buggy rolled past the red-clapboard Pugh house. Lily could almost hear that tiny voice saying, "Thank coo." Rubbing her hand over an aching shoulder, she remembered the feeling of those loving arms in that tight, heart-tugging hug. From beneath the dark fan of her eyelashes, she studied Green. He would give her the beautiful children she longed for and a home to rule as she chose.

Green's tone was gentler, placating when he spoke, "As Mrs. Green Bethune, your life will be such a constant social whirl that you'll have no time to think of little, unimportant people."

Lily well knew that as a married woman she could accomplish things with her life that a spinster could never do.

Green reined the horse in front of a large Greek Revival mansion. The first example of this style in the area, built by Dr. Levi Wellborn in 1839, it rose in temple-like grandeur with four massive round plaster-on-brick columns. A cantileveraid balcony ornamented the second story. "Do you like this style? The symmetry and graciousness wear well."

"Yes, I like the straight, clean lines of Miss Roxana Wellborn's house. The balcony without visible support is interesting. . . ." Her voice echoed stiffly in her ears. She hesitated. Her neck and shoulders ached as she tried desperately to accept this turning in her life. "If I had a house," she said slowly, "I'd want tall, round columns like this."

"You shall have as many columns as your little heart desires," Green beamed expansively. "All the way around the house if you want them."

Green continued to drive up and down the town looking at all of the magnificent houses. Riding along the heavily wooded area of Randolph Avenue, he stopped in front of the towering, Italian Renaissance mansion just completed by William Simpson. Earnestly, he pointed out the Gothic arches filled with wooden tracery around the veranda and the Gothic windows of the cupola. He began expounding on the air moat built around the lower level to keep it cool and moisture free, but Lily's eyes remained on the cupola. She could imagine Mrs. Simpson up there on the captain's deck watching for the arrival of Mr. Simpson's cotton boats. Green was disregarding what she had said about thinking of Harrison.

"I don't want this style house," she said softly. Her jaw pained sharply from clenching it. Desperately, she tried to focus her attention upon Green. They agreed upon a Greek Revival design with many white columns and a site on Randolph Avenue near the house built by Eufaula's first mayor, Dr. William Thornton. Driving slowly along Eufaula Avenue, they compared the beautiful homes and then returned up the hill to Barbour Hall.

Cordelia Edwards met them happily with her plans completed for the engagement party. Lily glanced over the guest list and mentioned several names her mother had not included.

"I meant to leave them off," Mama sniffed disdainfully. "I'll invite the cream of society—no social climbers."

Papa arrived at that moment and Green explained their house plans. Lily sat apart from them on a stiff-backed chair. The parlor was immaculate again, coolly formal. Their conversation flowed around her as if she were merely one more beautiful object in the room.

That night Lily dreamed that the boiler exploded on the *Wave*. Harrison's face floated in flames. Awakening drenched with perspiration, she tiptoed through her adjoining door into the sitting room. From the window seat she leaned out to the tiny balcony hoping to catch a cool breeze. Feeling someone behind her, she turned to see Emma who stood with her white gown glistening in the moonlight. Watching her silently, Emma waited, ready to help.

"Oh, Emma, do you think I'll ever get Harrison out of my mind and heart?"

"I don't know," Emma replied, sadly shaking her honey-colored hair that fell in a long braid. "I can't advise you, but I do understand how you feel." Her pale blue eyes ashine with compassion, she put her arm around Lily's shoulder.

Lily knew that her friend did indeed understand all too well. For this very reason, she found it difficult to discuss her problem. She feared hurting Emma's feelings. She could not voice her decision that she did not wish to become like her aunt.

The next morning Green asked in his most charming manner if he might borrow Prince. "I have business out the Montgomery Road, and I'd prefer going on horseback."

"Well," Lily cleared her throat. "I usually don't let anyone ride Prince except . . ."

"I'd take care of him. I like animals with spirit."

Limply, Lily agreed. Sighing often, Lily moved through the day of dress fittings numbly.

Cordelia Edwards, thoroughly enjoying herself with preparations for the engagement party, was too busy to talk with her daughter. Watching for a chance, Lily finally caught Papa alone.

"Oh Papa," she wailed, "shouldn't a bride be happy?"

He patted her awkwardly. "Brides are always nervous, honey," he replied soothingly.

"Papa, are you sure I can learn to love Green?"

"Just give it time, give it time. You see how eager he is to please you."

"Yes, he's charm itself, but does he really care about me?"

Distractedly, Papa mumbled that he must be getting to his office. "Things will work out, you'll see."

Lily sought solitude in the summerhouse. A happy little hummingbird brought memories flooding over her. In her mind's eye, she could see Harrison standing there, his usual vitality stilled. For one long moment that would remain forever locked into her heart, they had been joined in the wonder of one of God's tiny creations. She could almost feel his hand grasping hers. His touch had stirred her whole being. Sadly shaking her head, she hoped that one day she would share her joy in small things with a child.

That evening Green still had not returned. After waiting supper for an hour, they had just begun to eat when the ringing of horse shoes sounded in the drive. Jumping up, Lily hurried to the stable to be certain Prince received proper care.

Whinnying, her pet pushed against her, nipping his big soft lips hungrily at her empty hand. His saddle was in place. There was no sign of Green.

"Papa!" she ran toward the house screaming. "Papa, Prince came back without Green!"

Clare Edwards rushed to meet her. "Prince is used to no one but you," he said soothingly, "Don't you think he probably threw . . ." His voice trailed away and his darting eyes showed that he knew Green to be an experienced horseman.

"He rides to the hounds, and . . ." Lily began.

"Do you know where he went?"

"Out the Montgomery Road."

Edwards quickly organized a search. Foy joined the party without asking. Lily fumed because she could only sit home and fidget. For hours, they waited. Mama sat in the parlor, embroidering a linen handkerchief. Emma's sensitive fingers caressed the mother-of-pearl keys of the rosewood piano with the simple, soothing notes of Beethoven's moonlight sonata. Sitting, standing, pacing, Lily could not be still.

It was nearly midnight before she saw lanterns flickering through the silent darkness. Running through the yard toward the slow-moving, hushed men, she stopped and gasped.

Green lay on a litter. His face was deathly white.

"Papa!" she screamed. "Papa, is he?"

"No, no, dear," Papa hurried to meet her. "He's alive. But he's badly wounded. I've sent for the doctor."

Green was taken to his room. Lily was not allowed to go in. On the porch, she questioned Foy.

"He was shot in the back!" The child hopped from one foot to the other excitedly. "Oh, Sister," he whispered, "Do you think they might blame Captain Wingate?"

Lily sought a chair. "No, no, surely not," she swallowed. "Anyone who witnessed the duel would know that . . ." Lily thrust both hands into her brown curls and tore at her hair. She well knew that they were still close enough to the frontier for justice to move too swiftly. Many innocent men had been hanged.

"Are you sure he's far away?"

"Well, I thought—what's the sheriff doing with Prince?"

"Checking his hooves," the boy answered importantly. "He was out there doing all kinds of tracking and measuring."

For three days, Green remained near death. Lily sat on the porch nervously watching the comings and goings. Whenever she peered into his darkened room, he lay pale and still. Needing strength, she began to bring her Bible. Pulling the heavy rocking chair to the corner to catch every breeze, she started reading the Psalms. Whenever she read aloud to Mama, her attention was on her diction. At the church, she learned stories and maxims. Now in her need, she read searchingly. With her heart open, the voice of God began to come alive from the pages of her Bible.

Green at last regained consciousness. She spoke to him gently and uttered a thankful prayer. Back on the porch, she was stretching in the sunlight, relaxing taut muscles when Foy bounded up the steps.

"There's going to be a trial," he shouted, "as soon as they know if it's assault or murder."

"Shush Foy!" She motioned to quiet him lest Green hear. "What have you heard?"

"There's going to be a trial. They've arrested Mr. George Lorring!"

Unmindful of her dress, Lily sank to the steps, dropped her head in her hands, and sobbed. Weak with flooding relief that Harrison was not being accused, she knew with certainty that her heart would never change. The feelings that Green's illness had stirred were merely concern. She would always love Harrison. Through tear-dimmed eyes, she saw Foy standing silently before her. At last she realized he was thrusting something into her hand.

As she took the letter from Harrison, Foy turned without a word and fled. Her heart leaped, but then her hands began to tremble as she remembered her last letter to him. As she read words overflowing with love, she realized that he had not had time to receive her letter saying she could not marry him.

August 29, 1858

Apalachicola, Florida

My Sweet Darling Lily,

It is a miserable, dark, rainy Saturday night, and I am alone, thank goodness. The good people of Apalachicola must have retired, for I have not heard a foot fall on the sidewalk for over an hour. Silence reigns supreme save for the monotonous dripping of the water in the gutter. I like the stillness because it serves my purpose.

I have said I was alone, but beg pardon, not quite alone. I have two companions, my cigar—not a pipe this time—and a picture of a little blue-grayed beauty. For the last hour or two I have been puffing my cigar and talking to the little smoke person as though she were present, trying to tell her how much I love her, though I know it can't be told. I took the little hymnbook, hallowed by her touch, looked for a long time at the name on it, and read several hymns. I intend to read it regularly, and probably by the time I see you again will have read it through. It brings forth confessions of a sinner saved by grace and makes me feel at one with you in spirit.

You have made me the happiest man in the world by your letter, which assured me of your everlasting love and longing to be my wife. I received your letter in two weeks this time although it often takes five. I will not despair again, knowing that your love is true and I will hear again from you if only I will be patient.

It is very late, and my candle is burning low.

Good night.

I love you dearly.

With much devotion,

H. H. Wingate

Lily laid her head on the wicker table and sobbed as she never had before. The tender words pierced her heart. Stumbling, blinded by tears, she ran to the back of the garden. Struggling with her hoop, she sat down on the level, brick ha-ha wall. Dropping into the wide ditch, she was stunned for only a moment. She snatched her skirt from the wild blackberry briars, scrambled up the slope of the ditch, and ran into the meadow until she was sure no one would find her. Throwing herself on the ground, Lily beat her fists and sobbed. How had she ever let this wonderful man go? She had lost him forever.

When she could cry no more, she lay on the grass exhausted. Gradually she realized that no matter how lonely her life might be, she could never marry Green when she loved Harrison.

She left the meadow with strong resolve knowing that the family would be furious; however, the scene after dinner was far worse than she had ever imagined. She had waited until after the meal. Looking at her parents lolling in their chairs, too well fed to get up immediately, Lily stood shakily to her feet.

"You must listen to me," she said in a quiet, firm voice that turned their eyes upon her. "I know you love me and think you're planning my life for the best—no, wait, let me talk," she flung up her hand as they started to protest. "I've tried very hard to go along with your plans, but I simply cannot do it." Lily's cheeks were growing pale and she grasped the chairback until her knuckles whitened.

Emma sat clutching her fists, making no effort to hide the tears slipping down her cheeks. Lily looked at her with a shuddering sigh and resumed talking before anyone recovered from shock enough to stop her.

"I have tried to believe you know best," she repeated, "but every principle within me rebels. I cannot—will not—marry one man when I love another."

Mama fainted.

"Lily, you promised me you wouldn't . . ." Papa gasped.

"Yes, Papa, I promised." Lily compressed her lips. "I wrote Harrison that I could not marry him without your blessing. But I will always love him. I will not marry at all."

Mama's eyes fluttered and she moaned.

"You must not tell this to Green in his condition. We will not speak of it again until after the trial," said Papa firmly.

As the lurching stagecoach bumped over the road that wound up to Clayton, the county seat, Lily sank miserably into her corner. Nothing had changed. They were still putting her off like a child who would forget a whim and become docile again. Knowing that she could not go on like this, she shut her eyes to blot out their stern faces and poured her heart out to God. Acknowledging and confessing every sin of her young life, she began to breathe without the painful lump in her chest. A feeling of peace filled her. "Lord," she prayed, "I commit my life to thee."

She climbed down from the stage, filled with a new sense of strength. Tossing back her curls, she lifted her chin, ready to face whatever life brought.

The circuit court session dragged on for several days. Mr. Edwards and others who had been in the search party testified to finding Green Bethune lying face down, shot in the back, with a large portion, but not all, of his money missing and his papers scattered around him. A witness testified that Green Bethune stopped at the Mitchell residence to ask directions to the Montgomery Road. The witness admitted overlooking the fact that the other road, which appeared to head the same way, went to Lorring's house. Another witness gave evidence of seeing Bethune ride a small black horse up to Lorring's house and that later Lorring rode a large bay in the same direction by which Bethune had returned and taken the other fork.

On the third day in the courtroom, which smelled of

tobacco and oiled floorboards, Lily was called to the stand. The prosecuting attorney established that Green Bethune was riding her black horse. "Is it true, Miss Edwards, that your horse was wearing shoes?"

"Yes, sir," she replied. "I had him shod a few months ago."

"Is it also true that there is a distinctive split in the right front hoof?"

"Yes, sir."

"And this requires a different shoe?"

"Yes, sir."

"And can you positively identify your horse's tracks?"

"Yes, sir."

"Now, be certain, Miss Edwards. Were these tracks, which were observed, measured, and recorded at the scene of the crime, made by your horse?"

"Yes, sir."

"Please tell the court when you first saw your horse after Mr. Bethune left you in the morning of the day in question."

"At nine in the evening, I heard Prince cantering up the driveway. I found him at the stable completely lathered. He was very excited and riderless."

"Thank you, Miss Edwards. You may step down."

Lorring's stableman testified that the horse Lorring rode was a large, solid red gelding with a black mane and tail. He was unshod. The man identified the measurements of Lorring's horse's hoof, which corresponded with the tracks seen. The big bay had been found dead back in the swamp and identified.

Tension mounted and people whispered as the sheriff took the stand. Reared back in the chair, he matter-of-factly described how he had measured the tracks from the point where both horses went away from Lorring's house with the bay's tracks coming after the black's. He cleared his throat importantly and everyone leaned forward as he said, "At the point where the assault was committed, Bethune's horse was a little ahead of the one Lorring rode. The black gave a sudden spring forward as though the rider's control over him had ceased the moment when he had started by a sudden affright," he leaned toward the jury, "as from the firing of a gun."

The judge rapped for order.

"Lorring's horse, however, gave evidence of his being under control of his rider. You could readily tell that the bay was frightened because of the deep, though stationary impress from the hoof!"

Again the judge had to rap for order.

"Your honor," the prosecuting attorney said, "I am now ready to sum up this case. The conclusive evidence proves that George Lorring—"

"Stop him!"

"Don't let him get away!"

Lily's bonnet fell awry as she whirled toward the shouts. After a brief scuffle, the culprit was returned to the dock.

"Yes, yes, I shot him!" yelled Lorring, struggling against the men who held him by both arms. "But I only took back what was mine." With every eye upon him, he sneered, "It's that gentleman from South Carolina who is the thief!"

CHAPTER 10

"GREEN BETHUNE IS THE THIEF!" Lorring continued to shout. "I recovered what was mine!"

Rapping his gavel to no avail, the judge at last called a recess and cleared the buzzing courtroom.

When court reconvened, Green was called to the stand to identify the stolen property.

Lorring's lawyer deftly led him into giving a full account. "Is it not true, Mr. Bethune, that two days prior to the day in question, you met my client at the Chewalla Hotel and *failed* to pay him exactly the amount of money missing from your person?"

Green answered in a casual tone. "It is true that I met Mr. Lorring and paid him $9,600 for 186 bales of cotton."

"Please tell the court what this amounts to per pound."

"Ten cents."

Lily was puzzled and nodded when the judge challenged the line of questioning.

With reassurance that it was pertinent, the defense lawyer continued. "Is it not also true, Mr. Bethune, that as his cotton factor, you wrote to my client six months ago stating that if he would store his last fall's crop until you arrived, you would pay him twelve cents per pound?"

Green squirmed. He cleared his throat. "I did suggest. . .in the fall of 1857, the price had fluctuated from ten to eleven cents. I suggested to Mr. Lorring that because of the new power looms and increased cotton manufacturing in Lancashire, England, the price would probably go up. I said that if he would like to risk holding his crop, I would likely be able to pay twelve cents." He cleared his throat again. "Unfortunately, the market fell back to ten cents."

"Your honor, I would like to place this letter in evidence that Mr. Bethune made a definite agreement."

Lily stood as unobtrusively as possible, but her petticoats seemed to rustle loud enough for everyone to hear as she tiptoed from the courtroom. Seeking a shade tree and a cooling breeze, she did not want to hear the judge's decision. She had made her own.

In her parents' hotel suite, Lily faced them with a bright red spot in each pale cheek. "Papa, Mama, after hearing the evidence, I hope you see that Green is not the man for me!"

Papa's expression lacked understanding. "Lily, dear, you didn't wait to hear the decision. Lorring was found guilty of assault and robbery. Green broke no law." His voice croaked. "The letter was not binding—"

"Perhaps not," Lily interrupted, "but in breaking his word, Green broke Mr. Lorring. Time and again I've noticed him shaving principles that I believe in."

"Don't interrupt your father, Lily," Mrs. Edwards interjected sharply. "You know nothing of business. If a man is to keep great wealth and power, sometimes an end must justify the means."

"Not to me, Mama." Lily stamped her foot. "It is principle that matters. Down to as small an amount as a postage stamp!" Her voice rose angrily. Struggling with her temper, she spoke slowly, emphasizing each word, "I will not marry Green."

"What about principles of children obeying their parents?" Mrs. Edwards spit out the words sarcastically. "Of honoring thy father and thy mother?"

"I'm sorry, Mama. I respect you and I want to obey, but I can't keep being a child and a woman at the same time. I know you've planned my life according to custom, but I cannot do something just because everyone is doing it. I have to listen to a higher voice."

"What will our friends think?" wailed Cordelia. Sinking her chin on her chest, she sighed, "How will I ever face Laurie?"

Contritely, Lily realized that her mother actually appeared to be sick. She had to escape them, to be alone and cry. She started toward the door.

"Lily wait!"

Turning, she looked at Papa whose face was a frightening purple.

"You promised you wouldn't run away."

"No, Papa," she bowed her head and answered softly, "I realize you love me, and I love you. I would never run away."

The estrangement from her parents left Lily feeling weak and sick. Shedding angry tears, she felt that they did not really care about her or they would understand; yet, a growing part of her knew that they did care. Few words were exchanged in the stagecoach back to Eufaula. Subdued, Green said little. Watching him wince at the jolting, she knew the ride was painful. She dreaded their confrontation.

Thankful to be home again and out of her dusty traveling costume, Lily bathed and put on her coolest muslin. After giving Green ample time to rest, she tapped on his door and asked him to walk with her to the summerhouse.

Under the white lattice gazebo, she faced him with quiet resolve. Proud of her self-control, she eluded his reaching hands and spoke firmly. "Green, I've told my parents not to announce our engagement."

"Now, Lily-honey," he drew her into his arms, "you can't change your mind." He pressed a bearded kiss upon her lips.

Shaken, she pushed him firmly away. "Please, Green, no. Listen. Life with you would be fun. But surface attraction isn't enough. We are too different inside. I can't really give you my heart. You should marry a great beauty—like Elmira—someone to follow you without question. You don't really love me!"

Green looked at her intently, and his eyes showed that he sensed a change in her. He spoke without banner or calculated charm. "I've come to care for you a great deal more than you think. I meant it when I said I like a woman with spirit. Can't we give it a try?"

"No. I believe marriage is forever. Please, Green, don't make this harder. I don't know what's to become of my life, but I'm trying to commit it to God."

Groping through the smothering blackness, Lily crept up the narrow stairs, tiptoed through the attic, and climbed to the belvedere. The intensity of the darkness lessened only slightly when she emerged. Obscuring moon and stars, clouds enwrapped the glassed observatory. Suddenly lightning gashed the sky and thunder shook her high perch. Swirling, beating from all sides, the summer storm lashed her tower hideaway. Below her, the treetops danced madly. Dizzied and frightened, she looked up. Perhaps it was dangerous to be here, but Lily felt she must be alone. Watching the rain streaking the windowpanes, she ruefully reflected that the storm seemed pale compared to the one raging within her.

The evening meal had been an agony as they all tried to shake her resolve. She would not be swayed. Her parents were angry and disappointed with her Emma sat clutching her hands fearfully. Utterly dejected, Green said bitterly that he would be packed and gone the next morning.

Foy came to her side. He had sat silently through all of the recriminations that had been thrown at her. Now, he did something he had not done since he was a small boy; he kissed her affectionately on the cheek. He seemed suddenly tall as he put his arm around her shoulders and helped her to mount the stairs with a shred of dignity. At the door to her bedroom, he hugged her tightly.

Now as her sighs matched the moans of the wind, Lily remembered the admiring gleam she had seen in his eye. He had said nothing. As she watched the rain streaking the windowpanes, Lily smiled through her tears at the way her young brother had stood beside her. In the middle of the sleepless night, she had sought the solitude of the belvedere. Here she felt totally alone. She would remain so, for she had lost both men.

When at last the storm had spent itself, she sank to the floor and slept, exhausted.

Sunrise flooded the glass-enclosed room with pink and gold and awakened her to a new beginning.

"This is the day which the Lord hath made; we will rejoice and be glad in it." Lily repeated Psalm 118, verse twenty-four, through teeth clenched with determination. She went down the stairs to deal as best she could with her family and the new course she had decided for her life.

In the sweltering days that followed, Lily spent a great deal of time in the isolated belvedere reading. Guilt feelings tormented her. She exhausted herself going over and over the things that had been said and done. She muttered aloud the words she wished she had said from the beginning. One moment she would weep with the deep hurt that her parents had not tried to understand her feelings; the next surge of tears would come from the guilt of not being the obedient daughter they expected. She felt sorry for hurting Green. He had been a thoughtful suitor. There remained one thought from which she did not waver: she loved Harrison. But she had hurt him, too.

She flung angry, questioning prayers at God. "Why? Why?" She took her doubts to Him. "Dear Lord," she prayed, "I have sinned against everyone and against thee by putting myself first. I know that nothing I can do can save me from my sins, but I know that you have taken them all away by dying on the cross and rising again. I accepted thee when I was a child and thou came into my heart. Now as an adult, I want to commit every area of my life to thee." Filled with the presence of Jesus, she found peace to sustain her through the difficult days.

The tumult within her began to steady, but the longing for Harrison did not cease. Needing direction for her life, she began reading the New Testament.

Harrison seemed to be beside her one morning as she read the tenth chapter of Acts. She was transported from the summer-warm belvedere to the soft, spring night at prayer meeting when they had looked across the church and their eyes had met. Closing her eyes now, she could see him perfectly, sitting there so quietly, yet so vitally alive. She could remember the oneness she had felt watching his ready smile play about his always upturned lips. She could feel the warmth as his eyes expressed love that surpassed mere words. The preacher had been reading this same passage that she now held in her lap about Peter's vision on the rooftop. She had paid little attention that night as her eyes kept lifting to Harrison. Besides, the story of the sheet descending from heaven, filled with beasts and fowls and creeping things, was familiar to her from childhood. Now she read it thoughtfully.

"Rise, Peter; kill and eat."

"Not so, Lord; for I have never eaten anything that is common or unclean."

"What God hath cleansed, that call not thou common."

With mounting excitement, Lily read again of Peter's meeting with Cornelius, the centurion of the Italian band. When Cornelius fell at his feet to worship him, Peter commanded him, "Stand up; for I myself am also a man."

She began to walk about and read aloud. The familiar words spoke directly to her for the very first time as Peter was lifted from the ancient traditions that it was unlawful for a Jew to keep company with one of another nation.

"But God hath showed me that I should not call any man common or unclean," she repeated Peter's words over and over and then fell to her knees in prayer.

When she arose, she saw Papa leaving the house. She waved and called to stop him. Clutching the Bible to her, she ran down the endless flights of stairs and out across the yard, catching him just before he left.

"Papa, Papa, I must talk with you at once," Lily's eyes shone.

Mr. Edwards looked in surprise at the animated girl who had been listless and wan. Protesting only slightly that he should be getting to work, he let her drag him by the hand to the summerhouse. The leaves of the wisteria vine that shaded the latticed house were yellowing and dropping prematurely because of the drought. The flowers in the garden drooped their heads like sleepy children ready for a nap. In the midst of them, Lily's face and form were opening like fresh blossoms watered from the fountain springing up within her soul.

Waiting until he was seated comfortably before she began, she said excitedly, "Papa, I've been reading the Scriptures, and I really feel the Lord is speaking to me!" She spread her Bible before him on the wicker table and pointed out the passage.

Clare Edwards smiled at her indulgently as she read again of Peter's vision. Happiness that his daughter was herself again lifted the creases from his brow.

Without fully listening to her, he murmured, "Yes, of course I know the story of Peter's beginning to preach Christ to the Gentiles, but what does that have to do—"

"Papa, Papa, it's not just a story. God is speaking to us just as He did to Peter." She brushed back wisps of damp curls. "Listen to verses thirty-four and thirty-five, 'Then Peter opened his mouth, and said, Of a truth I perceive that God is no respecter of persons: But in every nation he that feareth him and worketh righteousness, is accepted with him.' " She smiled at her father triumphantly with her eyes sparkling and her whole being radiating happiness.

He looked at her quizzically.

"Don't you see, Papa?" she laughed. "It speaks to our ancient traditions of marrying within family groups and class. What matters with God is that a man fears him, serves him, and oh, Papa. . . " She jumped up and danced around him with brown curls bobbing and her skirt tilting and swaying. "Harrison is a dedicated Christian."

Edwards rubbed his hand over his head uncertainly and sighed. He took the Bible from her and reread the passage several times.

At long last, he raised his eyes to his glowing daughter. "Yes, I do see what you are saying. It is basic to building a lasting marriage that both partners believe the cornerstone to be faith in God. However," his voice broke and he looked at her doubtfully, "it is also important to be on the approximate cultural level."

"Yes, Papa," she agreed soberly, standing still and clasping her hands in front of her tiny waist. "That part is so wonderful. Our minds run on the same level—if not always in agreement, at least open to discussion. We are one in spirit, one in mind. All that remains . . ." She blushed at the remembrance of Harrison's touch.

"You have always had a deep faith for one so young," Clare Edwards said thoughtfully.

"Yes, Papa, I've believed as long as I can remember that Jesus is God's Son, that He is my personal Savior, but now I'm trying to grow, to make Him Lord of my whole life. I believe God's voice speaks to us in our minds and from the pages of the Bible to direct even our smallest problems of daily life. God cares about who we marry."

Mr. Edwards cleared his throat. "If you feel this strongly, I will give you my blessing to marry Captain Wingate."

Lily threw her arms around his neck, laughing and crying.

"Wait, wait," he pushed her back and looked anxiously into her face. "Don't get too excited. It will not be this easy to convince your mother not to consider your young man common."

"Yes, we have always thought of this as a problem in the early church," she said seriously, "but I've never shared Mama's view of people. I've never chosen my friends for what their name is or how long their family has had money. I like people for themselves, for what they think, for the ideas we can discuss." She paused and her dark eyes twinkled. "I find merely gossiping about acquaintances not only un-Christian but also boring." Her laughter trilled like a mockingbird.

Edwards chuckled, then nodded ruefully. "I should have understood. I should have realized that you have grown into a woman with a mind of your own. But how can I be certain Harrison will take care of you?"

"You can be sure because he is a sincere Christian!" The firmness of her voice and the calmness of her demeanor showed fully that she was no longer a vacillating child.

"All right, honey," he kissed her a fond goodbye, "I'll have a long talk with your mother tonight."

Happily, Lily gazed after him as he walked quickly away. He was late, she knew, but dear Papa always took time for her. Lily wandered through the garden singing, pausing frequently to savor the beauty. She breathed deeply at a bed of spicily fragrant lemon lilies. She could scarcely contain her joy. The blaze of crimson crepe myrtle blossoms, which defied the heat and drought by shining the brighter, made her smile and hug herself. Laughing at her foolishness, she kissed her hand for Harrison and stroked it across her cheek.

She wanted to remain in the cocoon of her daydreams, but with lagging footsteps she left the garden. Mama's back was better, and Lily had promised to help her make fringe for a counterpane. This was no time to disobey and make her angry.

Several times as the two women bent over the stitched bedcover, Lily opened her mouth to tell of her Scripture reading and her feeling that the Lord was leading her to marry Harrison. Each time she would merely murmur needless answers as Cordelia Edwards chattered on about the latest gossip. Mama gave time, just as Papa did, but she never gave attention. Whenever Lily tried to share ideas, the older woman would wait with a glazed look in her eyes, indicating that her mind was elsewhere while her little girl babbled. Lily tried to content herself with patience. Papa would reason with his wife tonight.

After several hours of bending over the counterpane, Lily was growing tired. Only then, did her euphoria diminish. Slowly, she counted and recounted the days since she had received a letter from Harrison. She had released him from his promise to marry her. There was no reason why he should answer the hurtful letter. He was a mature man, ready for marriage. He had probably found someone more willing than she.

At last Mama declared herself tired, and Lily escaped. She went to her bedroom. In her agitation the four walls seemed to press upon her even though the room was large and airy. Picking up her brass-bound lap desk, she headed toward the freedom of the belvedere. As she climbed the stairs, she reassured herself that Harrison still loved her. She would write again, telling him that Papa now gave them his blessing. Pursing her lips, she knew that she did not have her mother's permission, but she could wait no longer to write.

Foy had occupied the belvedere before her. His astronomy books littered the small table.

"Oh, Foy," she faltered, "I wanted to be alone to write to Harrison."

"It's about time you did," he snapped peevishly.

Surprised at his attitude, she replied pleadingly, "Can you get it off for me?"

"I don't know. Maybe not. The river is so very low, the boats cannot run regularly."

CHAPTER 11

"BOATS NOT RUNNING?" Lily looked at him in consternation. "Oh, Foy, I've been so wrapped in misery, I hadn't realized fall was upon us and time for low water."

"You know we haven't had rain and the cotton fields along the river bank are drawing moisture. This hot sun evaporates—"

"Oh, I know all that. I just hadn't thought," she interrupted, exasperated. "Foy, we've got to get a letter to Harrison. Papa's given permission."

"Yippee!" Foy yelped joyfully.

"No, wait," she shushed him with her hand, "Mama hasn't, but I must tell him as quickly as possible because," she bit her lip, "I wrote him that I couldn't marry him. I released him from his promise." She sat down suddenly and dropped her head so that her dark hair tumbled down in a curtain around her face. "He hasn't replied. It's been such a long time. Do you think he's found someone else?"

Foy made no sound. As the silence lengthened, Lily slowly raised her eyes. Foy stood twisting his book and shifting his big feet. His cheeks had lost their rosy roundness, but as she stared at him, the hollows turned beet red. His ears, standing out from his head, seemed almost to flap.

"What is it?" she gasped. "What do you know? It's been so long. What's happened?" She grasped his shoulders and shook him.

"I—I don't know anything," he stammered. "I don't know why you haven't heard. But it's not what you think."

She released him, gritted her teeth, and tried to be patient. "What then?"

"Well, you see, I. . ." he faltered, then finished in a rush. "I didn't send your letter."

"You didn't send my letter!"

"No, I, well, I didn't think you meant what you wrote. You were upset. I knew you'd change your mind." His lip curled. "I didn't want you to marry that Green."

"Foy, have you been reading all our letters?" she demanded.

"No, honest I haven't, Sister, but that day you'd been crying so much you looked wild. I decided. . .." He took a deep breath. "Yes, I read that one," he admitted. The tops of his ears glowed red. He continued slowly, "I went down to send it, but I just couldn't." He reached into a large book and solemnly handed her the letter.

Incredulously, Lily looked at the paper. Slowly, she unfolded it and scanned the hurtful words of refusal. Thankful that Harrison need never know of her parents' low opinion of him or that she had considered giving in to them and not marrying him, she laughed and cried as she shredded the letter. Leaning far over the rail, she threw the bits into the air.

"You're impossible, Foy, but I do thank you for interfering this time." She hugged him tightly and kissed his cheek. "Now, the problem remains of getting a letter to him. What are we to do?"

"I could take your letter down river to Columbia," he grinned happily. "The river seldom gets too low for steamers to reach there."

"Mama would never let you make a day-and-a-half trip on horseback. While I'm writing, go to the wharf and see if any boats are running."

He grinned and scampered down the stairs.

Lily sat down at the table, lifted the pin, and opened the secret drawer in which she kept Harrison's letters. Untying the pink ribbon that bound them, she skimmed his last letter. She reread the second paragraph:

> I have said I was alone, but beg pardon, not quite alone. I have two companions, my cigar—not a pipe this time—and a picture of a little blue-grayed beauty. For the last hour or two I have been puffing my cigar and talking to the little smoke person as though she were present, trying to tell her how much I love her, though I know it can't be told.

Lily smiled and kissed the letter. It made her happy to know that he daydreamed of her as she did of him. She read his last words aloud, trying to hear his deep voice speaking, "You have made me the happiest man in the world by your letter which assured me of your everlasting love and longing to be my wife."

Laying it beside her paper, she began to pour out her heart to Harrison.

September 4, 1858

Eufaula, Alabama

You surely have despaired of hearing from me, Captain Wingate, but I have just discovered that my last letter failed to get off to you. Now the river is so very low the boats cannot run regularly; and my heart aches that you may be long in receiving this, but I must share my joy.

Papa has given us his blessing! When can you come? Could we plan a Christmas wedding?

Lily put down her carved ivory pen and read over her words. She looked back at Harrison's letter and whispered his closing promise, "I will not despair again, knowing that your love is true and I will hear again from you if only I will be patient." A sob caught her voice. What if his patience had worn thin. It had been such a long time since either had had word of the other. She chewed her pen and then held it up to the light. She squinted into the tiny hole in the carved ivory at the picture of Jerusalem and thought for a long while before she dipped the pen into the inkwell and resumed writing cautiously.

Am I assuming too much? I have not heard from you in five weeks. Have you fallen in love with some Apalachicola lady and forgotten to write?

I tremble to think that I may have lost you in waiting for my parents' permission. I pray that our mail will get through and we will not lose each other forever.

No matter what happens, I will always love you and remain here waiting.

One piece of advice before I close—don't have the blues any more and quit smoking so much and I think you will feel better. Don't you wish I would stop talking so? I did love your letter as I will always love you. I shall stop for now and hope this may somehow wing its way to you.

Yours devotedly,

Lily

Rereading her letter, Lily frowningly realized that Mama had not yet been persuaded to accept Harrison; however, with Papa and Foy on her side, Mama would surely be won over. Lily sealed the letter and handed it to Foy with a confident smile when he emerged in the belvedere again after a quick trip to the waterfront. He had learned that a boat would be leaving at daylight tomorrow.

Foy brought her no letter. Was Harrison somewhere as lonely as she and wondering why he had not heard?

The next day, Mama remained in her bedroom admitting no one but her personal maid, Kitty. Although the family and the afternoon callers were given word that she was suffering greatly from rheumatism, Papa confided to Lily that he had discussed her ideas with his wife, but she was far from convinced.

Lily had spent the endless morning in the upstairs sitting room, nervously knotting macrame, jumping at each sound, hoping that her mother was about to emerge from her self-imposed isolation to talk with her. After Kitty took her noon meal on a tray, the tall girl reported to Lily that her mother did not feel up to seeing her. Now, with Mrs. Edwards even turning away callers, Lily could endure the house no longer. With Emma accompanying her, she went out into the stifling afternoon.

Heat rose in shimmering waves from the sun-baked road. As they walked, her hope that her mother would grant permission seemed also to shimmer like a mirage floating always before her, unattainable.

They walked down Barbour Street beneath China trees heavily laden with clusters of hard, brown berries. Ahead of them, crowds of tiny yellow butterflies, clinging jealously to a few small, damp spots, fluttered up reluctantly just out of reach of their swaying skirts. Turning left, they moved into the cooler, denser shade of Randolph Avenue. Mrs. Simpson waved as they passed her house. Lily felt too morose for idle conversation. She waved but did not slacken her pace. Emma stopped to talk with Mollie Simpson, and the two friends ambled along well behind Lily until they reached Fairview Cemetery. This quiet park suited Lily's mood. It was damp beneath the huge oaks and elms. Idly, she wandered by the tombstones, set at odd angles, that marked the graves of the early pioneers. Here and there clumps of roses, their sweetness intensified by the heat, seemed to heighten her feeling of infinite sadness.

Respecting her need for solitude, Mollie and Emma moved by her to speak consolingly to Mollie's twin sister, Elizabeth Rhodes. Countless times in the last year Mrs. Rhodes had placed flowers on her little Willie's grave. Sympathetic tears stung Lily's eyes. Fearing that if she began to cry she would never be able to stop, Lily turned from them. The twin sisters were a year younger than Emma, but both of them had beautiful homes and families. Lovely Emma had nothing. Lily must not let herself think about that. Sighing, she walked in the opposite direction along the circling driveway. She stood trembling on the bluff and stared unseeingly down the sheer drop to Cowikee Creek, far, far below, rushing to meet its destiny with the Chattahoochee.

After an unsettling supper for which Mrs. Edwards did not appear, Lily determinedly tapped on her door. Cordelia Edwards emerged grandly attired in black satin. Her hair was elaborately dressed in a youthful style of clusters of curls. Her expression was defiant, but her eyes were puffy and red.

Lily's dark eyes were wide with pleading as she softly begged, "Mama, please talk with me."

"Later," she snapped. "We have guests coming." She pursed her lips. "I've invited a group in for a musical soiree."

The next morning when Lily stepped out of her room, Mrs. Thornton was waiting with her carriage to take them to Mrs. Eli Shorter's plantation to spend the day. Even though their social customs dictated constant visiting, Lily readily saw that her mother was exerting extra effort to keep a crowd around them. As Lily politely greeted Mrs. Len Shorter and Mrs. I. G. Shorter, she could see Mama out of the corner of her eye supervising her prescribed inquiry after their health. Mama's smug smile emphasized the point that proper ladies visited in family groups of mothers with their daughters and daughters-in-law.

Just as they went into the dining room, beautiful Adriana, who had married Henry Russell Shorter, the handsomest of the Shorter men, tossed her long brown hair and asked, "When are you going to announce your engagement to that gorgeous Green Bethune? Someone else might snap him up."

Lily looked down at her plate, and stammered, "We, uh, decided not to marry. He's gone."

Cordelia Edwards popped her lips together. "This baby decided she wasn't ready to get married."

Blushing miserably, Lily toyed with her chicken.

"You won't find another good catch around here," Adriana laughed. "And you're not getting any younger."

Lily tried to change the subject, but the table talk constantly revolved back to marriage.

She sighed with relief when another group of ladies dropped in for a call later in the day. Conversation flowed freely without mention of her problems; nevertheless, she felt a lump of frustration swelling in her chest, threatening to explode like Foy's China-berry popgun.

Mama sat in the corner talking secretively with Mrs. Col. Chambers and Mrs. Van Hoose. Lily's breathing stopped when she sensed their subject. She strained forward to listen.

"Yes, my sister in Georgia has a delightful son," Mrs. Chambers gushed.

Desperately seeking escape, Lily discovered that Mrs. John Shorter was leaving to do a little shopping. Getting permission to ride back to Eufaula with her, Lily climbed into the carriage with her older friend and said, "I wanted to talk with you. I need advice on how to convince Mama that I want to lead my own life."

Her friend shrugged expressively and said nothing as her own mother climbed in beside them.

A swelling tide of emotion dashed Lily over the next six rocky days as her mother's dominance defeated her, and she turned more and more to attending the frequent church meetings that were a usual part of Eufaula life. Suddenly, revival broke out in the town. Lily and her friends attended morning and evening prayer meetings. It was a time of high emotion with crowds filling the church. Many came forward to the mourner's bench to confess their sins and need for God. Lily's heart overflowed as she watched the baptism of thirty at one service. Tears misted her eyes as her sweet voice joined the singing of the dear old hymn, "Amazing Grace."

Revival spread to churches of other denominations in the town, too. Lily's group visited everywhere. At a prayer meeting held at the Union Female College, Lily sat watching the shining faces of the school girls. She felt a growing conviction that God did indeed plan a choice of mate for each person just as surely as He destined other purposes for individual lives. Her guilt feelings from disobeying her parents were removed as she drew near to God in the worshipful atmosphere. Much as she longed to please them, she felt a calming assurance that the first thing in her life must be seeking God's will.

Even as Lily rejoiced that the whole town was stirred by revival, she prayed for herself and Harrison. With contrition, she recalled how she had asked God to guide her to the one who would share her faith. That early summer of her girlhood seemed so much more than a few short months ago. Had she really not expected an answer to that prayer? The answer had come so quickly that she had failed to recognize it. Did she have her chance only to lose it? Blinking back tears, she beseeched God that Harrison's heart would not turn cold with their long separation.

The revival opened Mrs. Edwards's heart. But not toward Lily's problem. It only served to keep her too busy for discussion. She was bent on visiting the poor. Dutifully accompanying her to carry gifts of food and clothing, Lily was shocked at seeing the privations of suffering humanity. Her mother kept puffing out her lips and reminding her to count her blessings.

One evening as she and Emma returned from a concert and dialogue at the college, they sat on the corner of the porch to catch the cooling breeze. Foy loped across the yard waving a small package over his head.

"You've got something, Sister. It came up with the wagons from Columbia."

Smiling at Foy's excitement, she did not reprimand him as he bent over her shoulder eagerly watching her open the package. She took out two photographs, one of Harrison and the other of a beautiful girl. Something else tumbled into her lap, but she snatched up the enclosed note without looking at it.

July 30, 1858

Mobile, Alabama

Ma très chère Lily,

I have been home to the family plantation, Greenleaves to visit. My mother was pleased with all I told her about you, but my sister, Jeanne, was quite surprised to hear I planned to marry you. This is a photograph of Jeanne. You will be great friends, I know.

I am also sending some sea moss. This moss is by some persons arranged in a highly artistic manner representing landscapes, animals, and so forth. I thought you might enjoy creating something.

I have not heard from you in a very long time. Please send me word that I may come to claim you as my bride before low water renders the river unnavigable.

Your obedient servant,

H. H. Wingate

Glancing at the date, Lily realized that the package had been weeks in transit, and that Harrison's assumption that they would be married was written before the long interval in which he did not hear from her.

Sharing the letter, she said, "It's odd, but his sister looks like a little French doll. Why do you suppose she was so surprised that he planned to marry me?"

"Maybe she was amazed that you would have him," replied Emma.

"But that makes him sound like a cad," protested Lily.

"Maybe he has girls in many ports, and she didn't expect him to ever settle down," contributed Foy.

"Oh, Foy, hush your mouth," she scolded laughingly, but as she idly turned the sea moss, she worried that he might be right. Maybe Mama's permission did not matter after all.

The next evening, they all attended a social given by their neighbors, Mr. and Mrs. Benjamin Franklin Treadwell. As Lily walked across the spacious grounds, she hoped Mrs. Treadwell's daughter, Adriana Shorter, would say no more about her expected marriage to Green. Normally, Lily enjoyed going to the beautiful house which had been designed by the great architect, St. Ledger. Master builders had constructed the tremendous house topped by a cupola with a captain's deck and balustrade.

As the family approached the grand mansion, Papa joined a group of men on the colonnaded veranda who were hotly espousing secession.

"Gentlemen, the South has lost everything by the Compromise of 1850," shouted William Lowndes Yancey. "Secession is the only resort!"

"I agree," thundered John Gill Shorter. "I hope our state will remain separated forever from the Union, as if a wall of fire intervened!"

Lily glanced toward them. Talk of war stirred every gathering now. Wondering what changes were to befall them, she shook her head, turned, and meekly followed the ladies crossing the porch to the beautiful entrance.

Framed by candlelight glittering through the imported sidelights and transom of the front doors, Mary Magdalen Treadwell beckoned the ladies to come inside the hall which was splendid with frescoes done by the famous mural painter, Sisk. A tall, erect woman of regal bearing and patrician features, Mrs. Treadwell fixed her snapping black eyes upon Lily and said loudly, "Adriana tells me you are not going to marry that handsome young man from the flower of South Carolina society."

"No, ma'am." Lily ducked her head. Her cheeks flamed as red as the damask draperies hanging from the gold cornices at the long windows. A group of her friends had heard the comment, and she kept her eyes on the heavy carpet of body brussels as she trudged across the room to join them.

"Hello, Lily, guess who I saw?" sang out Mary Elizabeth Brock. "Do you remember that mysterious riverboat captain you were making eyes at in prayer meeting last spring?" She began to laugh as Lily's face matched the draperies again. "Oh, I saw you. Don't deny it."

"Yes, I remember him," replied Lily, trying desperately to speak casually. "Where did you see him? Has a riverboat arrived?"

"No," replied Mary Elizabeth airily. "I just came down on the afternoon stage from Columbus, Georgia."

"You saw him in Columbus, then?" Lily pressed, wishing she could pounce on the infuriating girl and shake a direct statement out of her.

All of the girls giggled and chorused, "We thought you were interested in him!"

"Yes," Lily replied carefully. "He was the most interesting and dashing man I had ever met. Don't tease, Mary Elizabeth. Was he really in Columbus?"

"Oh, no," Mary Elizabeth tossed long, red curls and preened. "Didn't you know? I've been on a Grand Tour. I saw him in Washington City at a party for senators and congressmen. He was dancing with the most sophisticated beauty I've ever seen."

Lily's cheeks paled as the girl's words flung against them like cold water. Of course, his sister had been surprised that he would marry a silly schoolgirl when he knew accomplished international people.

"He is a mysterious man," contributed Elmira Oaks, interrupting her thoughts. The glossy-haired beauty knew that she was more sensuous and had more worldly knowledge than the rest. She strutted a bit, and said loftily, "Why do you suppose he's merely a riverboat captain? My Papa says that his family owns an old mansion built facing the Tombigbee River. It's just below Demopolis," she lifted her perfect nose, "and you know what it means to have a plantation in the Black Belt."

Lily knew well what it meant. The so-called Black Belt was a gently rolling prairie named for its fertile black soil. Within this crescent-shaped band covering nearly 4,000 square miles, were the largest and wealthiest cotton plantations. Some of the state's most beautiful homes with the most leisurely, gracious living were there.

"With all that," Elmira's knowing voice pierced her thoughts, "you'd think he'd be there. Do you suppose he's done something so bad that he's no longer received?"

"All I know," laughed Mary Elizabeth, "is that I saw him in Washington with a very beautiful woman!"

CHAPTER 12

"I PROMISE I'LL RETURN the favor," Lily sniffed as she stumbled through the darkness of the garden. She squeezed Emma's arm and tried to hold back the tears, but her cheeks glistened in the flickering torchlight. She wondered what she would have done had not Emma stepped into the circle of giggling girls and helped her escape.

Emma had taken her away by insisting that she must walk with her through Mrs. Treadwell's unusually landscaped grounds which had been inspired by Longfellow's garden at Cambridge. They easily hid themselves from view on the paths that were contoured to outline a seven-chorded lyre and slipped behind the red brick hothouse away from the party-goers.

"Have I lost him?" Lily sobbed on Emma's shoulder. "Did I delay too long in accepting him and make him turn to some woman who didn't have to think and do as she was told?" she wailed bitterly.

"Now, now," Emma soothed, "perhaps it's for the best. I guess Cordelia was right after all." Moonlight and shadows played tricks with her usually smooth face and etched a mask with rivulets of anxiety. "If he's not the gentleman you thought him, it's better to find out now."

"No!" Lily stiffened and drew away. "Emma! How can you say such a thing? I don't doubt Harrison's character! It's his inner self that matters to me, and I am sure of that. It's only," she sniffed, "that I may have driven him to the arms of another woman by not telling him so."

"But my dear, if his family owns such a large plantation and he's merely a riverboat captain there's a chance. . . ." Emma hesitated.

"I don't care about his family's wealth or social position," Lily declared emphatically.

"But if he's done something to disgrace them and the people he knows don't receive him. . ."

"But they do," she wailed. "He'd been home when he sent the package and he said his sister—"

"Was surprised that you'd marry him," Emma finished.

Lily fled from her and paced the dark-shadowed area at the back of the garden along the ha-ha wall. Suddenly she whirled and set her hoops rocking. She stormed at her friend who was pale and drawn with worry.

"No. No! I won't doubt him," she pressed her hands to her temples. "I'm not a child anymore. I won't be told what to think. I won't be a respecter of persons. Harrison stands as a man after God's own heart. He is rich toward God. That's what matters to me!"

Hot, dusty September days inched by as Lily paced out her frustrations in their drought-stricken garden. She seemed to be holding her breath in an agony of waiting. She would not be shaken in her trust of Harrison, but over and over she asked herself if she had grown up too late.

One afternoon as she sat in the latticed summerhouse staring at a book, pretending to read, she sensed a presence before she heard a step. Whirling, she flung her hand to her throat and gasped.

He came striding toward her. His white suit glistened brightly in the glaring sun, making her squint to see if her eyes could confirm the song her heart was singing. Standing shakily, she stretched out her arms with a joyful cry.

Harrison enfolded her in a strong embrace. Shielded from prying eyes by the drooping, yellowing wisteria vines, they clung to each other. His mustached mouth sought hers. Warmth and peace erased her pain, and she joyfully knew she had been right not to doubt him. His cool, smooth cheek pressed hers as she caught her breath, laughing and crying.

"How in the world did you get here?" she exclaimed at last. "I wasn't expecting to see you because the boats are running so seldom."

"I came down from Columbus, Georgia, on the stage. I've been across the country." He smiled adoringly and dropped a kiss on the top of her head. "It seems forever since I've heard from you. My mail hasn't caught up. You see I've been to Washington City."

"Yes. I'd heard. I didn't know riverboat captains were part of that social scene." Her voice lowered at the remembrance, and she dropped her eyes to her twisting hands. "I heard you were there dancing with a beautiful woman." She suddenly felt hot, sticky, and unkempt in her simple muslin dress.

Chuckles burst forth as he threw back his head and enjoyed a hearty laugh. "How news does travel!" He smiled mischievously and tweaked his mustache, obviously savoring her jealousy.

Lily looked up at him. He had never been as handsome as he was in his white naval uniform. His twinkling eyes were wide with candid innocence and infinite tenderness; yet, his tanned face and strong body were unfailingly masculine. Her dark, soulful eyes questioned silently.

"I had business in Washington, very successful, I might add." Grinning, he dropped his teasing tone and explained, "The beautiful lady in question was Senator Atherton's wife."

He was obviously eager to share his business affairs with her. He drew her to the wicker settee, and they sat holding hands and talking.

"A great many lives have been lost," he said earnestly, "to say nothing of four vessels from my family's steamship line alone. So for the past year I've been captain of one of our riverboats to see what could be done." He paused to see if she understood. "I don't like to brag about my family's holdings. We have other boats on the Tombigbee River and a rather large cotton plantation south of Demopolis. I'm certain Green told you all about my background before he introduced me into your family."

"No." She shook her head solemnly. "Green told us nothing." Her face was full of wonder as she said quietly, "I thought you merely Captain of the *Wave*."

Harrison's dark eyes searched her face incredulously.

Lily nodded at him with a tremulous smile. She watched his face as the realization spread over it that she had thought to give up all luxuries of life for him. Adoration for her filled his eyes, and he kissed her tenderly, then with a passionate strength that told her she need never worry about another woman again. His life would be completely dedicated to her as her life was to him.

"Well, anyway," he cleared his throat as he made himself pull away and said in an emotion-husky voice, "I've tried to introduce safety precautions, as I had told you, but the real problem is not on the steamboats, it's the river."

"The treacherous Chattahoochee," she murmured. Relaxing in the circle of his arms, she wanted to listen, to share his concern; yet, her mind pirouetted to the counterpoint of his deep voice against the melodies of the pines plucked by the fingers of the wind.

"Yes," he continued eagerly, "The Chattahoochee is full of snags, rocks, sand bars, low bridges. It's difficult to induce Congress to provide funds for clearance of the channel. That's what I hoped to accomplish in Washington." He spread his hands. "But, enough of what's kept me away. What have you been doing? Have I waited long enough for your parents to forget the embarrassment of the duel? Pray tell me you are ready to set a date for our wedding."

"Yes, yes," she roused herself, pleased that Harrison had never doubted her. Ruefully reflecting upon her past immature behavior, she breathed a thankful prayer that Foy had not sent her letter of refusal and that Green was out of their lives. Harrison need never know what problems his being too humble to speak about his family's status had caused. "Papa has given his blessing," she took a deep breath. "Mama will soon be persuaded now that you have returned." She shook back her hair and smiled up at him, eyes sparkling, "I'll talk with Mama this afternoon. Can you come back for supper?"

"Yes," he answered simply, and lifted her clenched fists to brush kisses across them.

"I promise to have them prepared this time," she laughed. "You may ask Papa again formally for my hand. Then we will tell them our wedding plans."

"I wish tonight could be our wedding supper." Again his voice was husky.

Lily's laughter tinkled merrily. "Give me a little more time. I must have a wedding gown that will make you proud of your bride."

"I'll always be proud of you. Would six weeks be enough time for you? By then I could arrange my business to allow for a long honeymoon."

"Yes," she answered firmly.

"I can't wait to take you to meet everyone." Harrison's face shone with happiness. "You'll especially love my sister, Jeanne. Everyone says she is very much like my French grandmother."

"French?" Lily lifted quizzical eyebrows.

"Yes. Didn't you know Demopolis was settled in 1817, by Bonapartists exiled because of their claim to the throne of France?"

"Well, I've heard about the Napoleonic exiles, but. . ." she shrugged at her lack of knowledge.

"Yes, well, the refugees' attempt to grow olives and grapes failed. Everything is planted to cotton now, but the riverport of Demopolis is still referred to as the 'Vine and Olive Colony.'"

"That's why you sometimes speak French," she laughed.

"It slips out," he grinned. "I hope you won't mind being out on the plantation. Planters don't build homes in town as much as they do here because our black Canebrake mud makes the roads practically impassable during the rainy months of winter and spring.

"I'll love being in your family's home. Wherever it is," Lily said softly, still scarcely daring to believe her happiness.

"I think you'll like Greenleaves. The house looks rather impressive from the river. It's set on a high, white limestone bluff. It was built in 1832 in the plain, Federal style. It was red brick when I left, but by the time we get there I may not recognize it. When I told my mother I was marrying a city girl, she started pestering my father to add a columned front portico and paint everything white to make it the fashionable Greek Revival style."

"I can't wait to see it," she laughed. Joyfully, she looked across the garden. Her eyes focused only on spots of beauty and color. Thinking that all of her problems were behind her, she blurred the things that were withering, dying.

They lingered long in the summerhouse and parted reluctantly even though it would be for only a matter of hours.

Lily immediately went to search out her mother. She was firm in her resolve to convince her that she should marry Harrison without telling her of his wealth and prominence.

Learning that Cordelia Edwards was visiting the sick, Lily ran lightly to the stables seeking release from pent up energy and fortification for her nerves. Whinnying eagerly, her spirited horse pranced and nuzzled her. Quickly, she saddled Prince and slipped out through the meadow before anyone could see her. She wanted to be alone. She eased her weight into the sidesaddle and held on tightly as long-legged Prince loped away.

Hatless, dark curls streaming behind, she let the horse run unchecked until they reached the riverbank. Lily jumped down to give Prince a rest and feed him a handful of sugar. Standing on the edge of the cliff, she looked down at the Chattahoochee sunk to its summer level eighty feet below the bridge.

Fancifully, she shook her finger at the thin, blood-red stream lying docilely between the rocks. "You didn't beat me," she said with her eyes twinkling merrily. "You won't come between us again."

When she returned to Barbour Hall, she found her mother in the wide central hallway of the house seeking a breeze. "Mama," she said firmly, "the time has come for us to talk."

"It's too hot, baby," Cordelia Edwards lolled on the horsehair sofa fanning listlessly.

Calmly, knowing she would neither be put off nor driven to tears, she replied, "No! Harrison is here. He's coming for supper. I must talk with you, now." She looked down at her and softened her tone. "Mother, I love you and respect you. Everyone in town sings your praises as they never will mine. . ." Pinned to the marble checkerboard floor by the piercing, arrogance of her mother's gaze, she faltered and her voice trailed away.

Cordelia Edwards sat with her head thrown back, her nostrils flaring, and her lips pressed firmly together.

Clearing her throat, Lily shuffled her feet. "We just don't look at life the same way." She shook her head. "And I guess we never will, but two people can't be exactly alike. It doesn't matter if you like red and I like green," she shrugged. "I've got to live my life as I feel God leading me. I can't be an adult and a baby at the same time."

Cordelia's darting eyes had the frightened look of an animal seeking escape. "I guess that is what I wanted you to do," she admitted. She pinched back tears. "But I'll always think of you as my baby."

"I can't be your baby any longer." Lily's voice was cold as she carefully controlled her temper.

Cordelia's face crumpled. The cloak of haughtiness fell from her shoulders, and she began to cry.

The sensitive girl hovered helplessly over her weeping mother as the sawing blade of her words severed the threads between them. Tears sprang to her eyes as she watched her mother's pain with a sudden stab of realization that the birth-cut between them had been made with a swifter, sharper knife.

Dropping to her knees, Lily gathered her mother's nervously flitting hands in hers. "Mother, I can't be your baby," she said tenderly. "I want to be your daughter. Two women together."

Cordelia began to laugh through her tears. She took her daughter's wet cheeks in both hands, and they kissed each other in loving embrace.

With strong conviction Lily knew that she would reverence and obey her mother when she could, but she would never again be cast down broken-spirited or feel herself a terrible child. Suddenly into her mind popped approving words, "Children, obey your parents in the Lord: for this is right." She laughed gently as she remembered how Ephesians six had amplified the commandment.

"Mama," she lifted her shining face and said brightly, "let me show you what I showed Papa." Lily ran to get her Bible and spread it before her mother. Carefully she explained her beliefs as she had to her father.

For once in her life, Mama gave her full attention. She pursed her lips and made no comment as Lily talked. When Lily finished they sat with silence lengthening.

At last Mrs. Edwards sighed. "I don't see it that way. This Scripture does not say to me what it does to you. I've only tried to do what I think is best," she spoke with an unaccustomed whine. "To provide you with a husband who is your social equal."

Lily waited quietly. She wished that she knew how to convey to her mother the joy she received from knowing her place in heaven was secured by faith in Jesus' sacrificial death and resurrection rather than through keeping laws and doing good works. Sensing that she could press her no farther, she held her breath and waited.

Mrs. Edwards looked at her for a long time. Sighing heavily, she said, "If you are determined to have your own way, I won't oppose your marrying Captain Wingate."

Dancing light sparkled in the prisms of the chandeliers above the long dining table and glittered over the blue satin gown of the radiant girl who sat as the center of attention. Mama and Papa had never been more charming. The cook had produced such an elaborate meal that Lily knew all of the servants must be whispering about her romance. The best tablecloth of Italian lace was laid over the gleaming mahogany table. In the center a silver epergne lifted a pyramid of fragrant pink roses and ferns above the heads of the diners. On either side a tall, five-branched silver candelabra held more lighted tapers aloft. In this festive atmosphere, conversation fluttered like a butterfly over pleasant generalities.

After the meal the family moved to the parlor for coffee. Harrison cleared his throat. His eyes sought Lily's. She reassured him with a smiling nod. "Sir," he began and cleared his throat again. "Sir, may I formally ask for your daughter's hand in marriage? I love her very dearly and promise you that I will dedicate my life to caring for her."

Clare Edwards reached up to pat Harrison's shoulder. "Lily assures me that you will," he smiled. "Her mother and I give you our blessing."

Foy whooped and then with new-found manhood solemnly shook Harrison's hand.

For once in her life, Cordelia Edwards sat quietly, saying nothing; but a strange smile quirked her lips. Emma looked quizzically at Lily, then shrugged, and served the coffee with a sigh of relief.

As Harrison reached for Lily's hand and squeezed it tightly, she spoke in a strong, sure voice, "We want to be married the first of November."

"But," Mama protested, suddenly coming out from her private thoughts, "that gives us so little time to get ready. A Christmas wedding would be so much more elegant. Wait 'til then," she said firmly.

"But Harrison can take time off for a honeymoon in November . . ." Lily began hesitantly.

"I would like to end our trip by taking her to my

family's plantation for Christmas. All of my brothers and sisters will be returning to Greenleaves for the holidays," he said politely yet confidently to Mrs. Edwards who acquiesced reluctantly. He turned to smile into Lily's eyes. "Mother's prized camellia garden will be blooming then, and she will take such delight in showing it to you."

"How lovely!" Lily declared in excited anticipation of the new worlds opening to her. "Then we must make it the first of November."

Her parents nodded in agreement; however, their fixed smiles were tinged with sadness.

Harrison noted their emotion and said gently, "I promise not to take her away from you all of the time. I thought next spring we'd start building a home in Eufaula."

Joyful cries met this announcement and everyone began talking at once. Tears of happiness shone in Lily's eyes as plans were made.

When at last she followed Harrison to the porch, she whispered, "I hate for this day to end."

"Many more happy days will begin," he smiled. "We can also build a home anywhere else that strikes your fancy. There is one thing I would ask though," he interjected seriously and looked into her eyes pleading for understanding. "I find I thrive on the challenge of the river. I want to continue to spend part of my time on the steamship line."

"Of course," Lily agreed. "I know you could never sit around idly."

Blissfully happy days filled the next week. The house buzzed with activity as the servants polished each spot and then shined it again. Plans were made for an engagement party. Emma was everywhere supervising preparations. She wore a constant smile as her loving heart overflowed with gratitude that her darling Lily would never know the loneliness that she had been fated. To Lily's satisfaction, Cordelia Edwards's guest list excluded no one.

The party was a glorious affair. Mary Elizabeth Brock came in nodding, "I told you so." Elmira Oaks tried to start whispers, but no one paid any attention. A few times as she milled about greeting friends, Lily overheard her mother telling people that Harrison's family included French aristocrats and bragging about his recent trip to Washington. Ruefully she realized that Mama had known, after all, who he was before she gave her blessing. Mama would never change, but Lily tried not to mind.

The next day, Harrison bade Lily a reluctant farewell. "The rapid changes on the river due to the extended drought have caused another disastrous wreck," he told her. "I must see what can be salvaged and settle several other business matters before I return."

"How will you go?" she asked, walking with him as far as the gate.

"There's a small boat, the *Peytona*, leaving immediately. It should get me there—and back," he assured her with a confident smile.

As he went striding away from her, Lily gazed after him, memorizing the way he walked. There was much to do before he returned. Resolutely she started toward the house, then went back to the gate for one last look down the hill, fighting a feeling of bereavement.

CHAPTER 13

"WHERE IS THE MYSTERIOUS GROOM?" Elmira Oaks breezed into Lily's blue and white bedroom unannounced.

The circle of bridesmaids, who were clustered around the high, rosewood bed to admire the lustrous white satin wedding gown spread across the counterpane, parted to admit Elmira.

"Isn't this the most beautiful thing you've ever seen?" squealed Mary Elizabeth Brock.

"She'll look like a dream," agreed Elmira airily. "But really, I thought Captain Wingate was due back a week ago. I wanted to give you a party."

Angry with herself that Elmira made her blush, Lily stammered, "He's—he will be back soon. He had business—"

"This is the prettiest part," interrupted Cousin Octavia. Ignoring Elmira, she directed their gaze to the ropes of pearls that fell in double scallops from below the tiny waist.

"I think I like the sleeves best," admitted Lily with a sudden shyness. "You'll see what I mean when I wear it. I love the way the petals float." She smiled at her plump-cheeked cousin who had come for a two-week visit.

The girls chattered and giggled at once, over the lovely bridemaids' dresses. As maid of honor, Emma would wear a slightly deeper shade of lavender taffeta than they. Creamy lace underlaid the dainty scallops of the necklines and dipped between the deep scallops of the hemlines.

Lily tried to relax. She had not realized that she was so tired. The past few weeks had been exhausting as they prepared for the wedding and packed the huge trunks in readiness for the extended honeymoon trip. She had not heard from Harrison and did not know how to write to him, but she had been too occupied to fret even though he was overdue. Now, Elmira's caustic words made her long for the security of his arms. Wrapped in the warmth of his embrace, she had blotted out what Harrison had tried to tell her about rocks and sand bars and wrecks. They had been mere words, challenges for him to overcome. Now they protruded into her mind as cold, hard foes.

As the group started downstairs in search of refreshments, Elmira turned to Emma. "Do you really think he'll make it back? There hasn't been a boat up river in weeks."

Emma glanced behind her, hoping that Lily had not overheard the remark, before she replied with false assurance. "Of course, he'll get here!" Then she amended, "You know low water is seldom a problem below Columbia." She hesitated, her smooth cheeks reddening, "Well, I'm sure there are times when it's difficult to reach Columbia by boat, but but he will be here the day before the wedding for rehearsal, I'm sure."

"Even if he gets to Columbia, it's a long way away." Elmira tossed her dark mane.

The seeds of doubt sewn by Elmira, watered by weariness, began to grow. That night Lily awakened from a dream-troubled sleep. She went to stand by the window and stare at the stars. Had anything happened to Harrison? She brooded, nervously twisting the curtains. What if he could not get back by the third of November, their appointed wedding day? Something stirred and Emma was beside her.

"Don't worry," the older girl whispered. "Everything will work out. Elmira's just a troublemaker. I'm sorry she got *you* started worrying."

Lily looked at her in surprise. The slight inflection Emma placed on her words told Lily that her friend had already been worrying. Although she could not see her clearly in the moonlight, Lily sensed she was in tears.

"Lily, dear," Emma breathed a shuddering sigh, "you know that life on the Chattahoochee is fraught with danger. If something has happened to Harrison, you have known a great love. That can sustain you for the rest of your life, as mine has." She drew back into the shadows and wept in broken sobs.

"Emma, Emma, don't talk like that!" Lily grasped the sleeves of her white muslin nightgown and shook her until her long braid flopped. "Nothing has happened to Harrison. He *will* be here!" she shouted.

She gulped a sigh and whimpered, "I'm sorry, but Emma, he will come." She wiped her eyes and got hold of herself with difficulty. "Dear Emma, your life isn't over." Lily hugged her tightly. "You mustn't say that. Maybe it was for the best that you didn't marry your love. God works all things together for the good to them that love Him and are called according to His purpose. He has a task for each of us. You don't know what lies in store for you if you're ready to serve Him. You can be sure He has some plan for your life."

"No," Emma shook her head. "I don't think that He takes notice of me at all. But I so want your life to be special."

Returning to bed, Lily stared for endless hours at the web of the macramé canopy outlined in the moonlight. Remembering her words of consolation to her friend and the calls of the missionaries during the revival, she wondered if she had foreshadowed her own destiny. Was she to give her life for service in India as they had done?

As the month drew to a close and all of her preparations lay completed, Lily began again to climb to the belvedere where she was at one with the brilliant blue of the clear, October sky. Daily she searched the Scriptures for wisdom. Ruefully she reflected that she should not have let her joy and the busyness of her life distract her from daily seeking power by reading God's Word.

One evening she sat at her roll-top secretary writing in her journal. "October 31, 1858. Still no message from Harrison. I pray that I may accept whatever comes."

Restlessness overwhelmed her, and she put down her pen and climbed to the belvedere. Clouds scudded across the sky. As she stepped out onto the deck, simultaneous lightning and thunder shook her and made her hang onto the balustrade. Lashed by the wind, her long, brown hair plastered by the rain, Lily wept out her anxiety.

November dawned cold and gray. Wrapped in a heavy shawl, Lily trudged up the stairs to her solitary sanctuary. Heavy shrouds of rain clouds pressed down upon the belvedere. The whole world seemed filled with rain, but the Chattahoochee rose a sparkling stream far, far away in the mountains of eastern Georgia. It must be fed a great deal of rain before it strengthened and stirred again into its mighty self.

Harrison should have been here long before this. The time for rehearsal had come and gone. She knew that everyone in the house was whispering behind her back that the wedding should be postponed. With anxious eyes, she searched the horizon for a puff of smoke that would signal the small boat's arrival.

Around noon, she had returned to her lookout when she saw Foy loping across the lawn waving his arms like a scarecrow in a windstorm. He was shouting, but the wind whipped his voice away. Running pell mell down the endless flights of stairs, she met him halfway, in the upstairs hall.

"Sister! Sister!" he screeched. Gasping for breath, he could not get out his words.

Tear streaks on his face made Lily's knees give way.

"King's Rock," he gasped. "King's Rock, Sister!" He collapsed at her feet, buried his face in his arms, and sobbed.

Lily sank to the floor beside him and stroked his hair, his ears. She knew all too well about King's Rock. It lay waiting treacherously, sometimes visible, sometimes not, in one of the most dangerous stretches of the Chattahoochee. The channel narrowed twenty miles north of the town of Chattahoochee, Florida. The anxious river rushed by the rocks at a great rate of speed toward the rendezvous at the town where the Chattahoochee married the Flint. Grief was common at King's Rock where steamer after steamer met its fate.

Emma emerged from the bedroom and stood over them, her face pale, her hands clutched together.

Looking up at her, Lily whispered, "Oh, Emma, I've prayed I could accept whatever came, but I was expecting an answer I wanted to hear." She tried to lift Foy's head. "Foy, dear, tell me. Tell me."

Fighting for control, the boy wiped his sleeve across his face. "I," he sniffed. "I went to the waterfront to wait. I knew Captain Wingate would surely arrive today." His voice broke again. "Wagons and carts came in from Columbia," he resumed shakily. "The water is so low. The paddlewheelers can't make it beyond there. The goods were unloaded and they brought the news that the *Peytona* struck King's Rock." He buried his face again.

"Was it grounded or. . . ."

With difficulty, Foy straightened up and related the events. "The *Peytona* went smashing into King's Rock! Totally wrecked. She sank! When the wagoners passed by," Foy swallowed convulsively, "they saw pieces of the *Peytona* floating—"

"Surely there were survivors?" Lily gasped.

"Yes, but they didn't know who. It was storming and people washed overboard. Some were lost trying to save others. And you know how Captain Wingate. . . ."

Cordelia Edwards appeared and wrapped her children in her ample arms, murmuring soothing words. Kitty stood behind her, wailing loudly.

"Hush, Kitty," she commanded quietly. "Emma, start sending out word to the guests that the wedding will be—"

"No!" Lily shouted. "No, Mama, I won't believe Harrison's dead!"

"Of course not, dear," she soothed. "We'll merely postpone the wedding. If he takes another boat and makes it past Columbia, there's still Purcell's Swirl. In such stormy weather, paddlewheels are damaged in the whirlpool. You know he can't get here in a day."

Papa came rushing up the stairs. Deep lines in his face told Lily he knew about the accident. As he threw his arms about her stiff shoulders, she cried out, "Oh, Papa, do you know about survivors?"

"No, dear, I've heard no names. We can only pray Harrison is safe. But, Lily, you must realize he can't get here by boat. A man at the wharf said that the water is so low south of here that you can wade across the river at Fort Gaines. Your mother is right. You must postpone the wedding." He jerked his head meaningfully toward Emma.

"Maybe," Lily admitted sorrowfully. "But, Emma, don't do anything yet." She stood up. "Please. Give me a little time alone." She turned and climbed the attic stairs slowly, like an old, old, woman.

Emerging in the belvedere, she collapsed on the floor with her head on a chair. Her tears would not come. Cold, numb, she huddled alone. For long, agonizing moments, she clung to the chair.

At long last, she raised her head. She was not alone. There was one to whom she could turn. Jesus promised His followers they would never be alone. His Spirit was always there waiting alongside to comfort, to strengthen if only one asked.

She stepped out into the cold wind and lifted her face to the sky. "Oh, Lord," she prayed, "If it be thy will, let Harrison be alive. I know that Thou dost love us and take care of us. I won't worry anymore. I'll leave it with Thee."

Shivering, but warmed inside, she stepped back into the glassed enclosure. She sat holding her Bible and whispered again, "I'll leave it in your hands."

As peace sent her blood flowing again, she opened the worn book to Acts ten. She could not put words to her prayers, but the Holy Spirit interceded for her and as she read God's Word, He seemed to be speaking quietly, clearly in her mind as He had spoken to Cornelius and Peter. She knew with calm assurance that Harrison was not dead. She read on in the second chapter of Ephesians, "For he is our peace, who hath made both one."

When she returned to her anxious family below, she was so strong in her convictions that they could not dissuade her. Even though all of them went about muttering under their breath that it was against their better judgment, they continued the wedding preparations.

On the morning of November third, Lily slowly, deliberately stepped into her widest hoop. The wedding was not scheduled until three in the afternoon, and Emma tried to get her to wait; but she wanted to be dressed and ready. Shaking her head sorrowfully, Emma lifted the lustrous satin over Lily's head, and it settled like a cloud around the slim girl.

Lily watched in the cheval glass while Emma fastened the loops on the satin buttons up the back and the gown closed tightly around her tiny waist. Lily adjusted the flounce of illusion across her shoulders and ran aching fingers along the scallops of pearls embroidered over the bodice. The girl in the mirror looked back with a white satin face and eyes of round, black coals.

"Don't you love the sleeves?" Lily said in a small voice and tried to make the girl in the mirror and the girl straightening the deep flounce around her feet smile. She lifted her arms and the sleeves, fitted to the elbows and then spreading from a ring of pearls into eight petals, floated to her wrists.

Emma laughed softly. "You are a beautiful bride!"

Carefully covering herself with a gray flannel wrapper, Lily compressed her hoops to negotiate the narrow staircase and climbed once more to the belvedere to wait.

Cold and tired, she sat until nearly noon. Passing her hand across her weary eyes, she saw a lathered horse plodding up the hill. When the rider dismounted and started running toward the house, his swinging hands assured her it was Harrison.

Floating down the stairs, she cast away the flannel wrapper. It did not matter if he saw her wedding gown before the ceremony. He must know the depth of her faith in him. He bounded into the entrance hall and swooped her into his arms before her feet touched the last steps. Flinging herself toward him, she laughed and cried.

Kissing her face, her hands, her hair, he murmured words of love and apology. He tried to explain about the accident and his long trip overland.

"Never mind. You're here," she laughed, looking into his eyes that seemed to be sagging in a face stained from the horseback ride. There were streaks of red dirt on her dress, too, but the marks only spoke of their dedication to each other.

After Mrs. Edwards had overseen the careful removal of the dirt from the gown, Lily had only to don her gossamer veil. Held by a crown of blossoms over her brown hair, it misted around her clusters of long curls. She stood ready, waiting while her groom prepared.

Like lavender butterflies, her bridesmaids fluttered around her. Proceeded by the stalwart Emma, she stepped lightly down the church aisle on the arm of dear Papa. At the altar, Harrison waited, his eyes alight with love.

As the minister's words, "What God hath joined together, let no man put asunder," were sealed with a kiss of commitment, Lily and Harrison began a life of joy which God has promised those who serve him.

In the happy years that followed, Lily and Harrison were filled with the calm assurance that God walked with them through the trials and challenges of life. Often Lily accompanied Harrison on his travels. Wherever they went, they found ways to spread God's love to those they met, and when she chose to stay home with their children, the presence of Harrison's love remained with her. Secure in the commitment of their Christian marriage, they were one in Christ. Never again could the river come between them.

Travel with Lily and Harrison Wingate in Jacquelyn Cook's exciting sequel, THE WIND ALONG THE RIVER as war changes their lives when the *Wave* is impressed into the Confederate Navy. Emma finds her life beginning as she looks into Jonathan Ramsey's dark and laughing eyes.

ACKNOWLEDGEMENTS

When I climbed to the belvedere and looked down on Eufaula, Alabama, as beautiful today as it was in the era of this story, I was transported back in time and could feel the warm breath of my characters. Showing me through the elegant mansion, Douglas Purcell, historian, editor, and Executive Director of the Historic Chattahoochee Commission, made the history of the area come alive. He took me to Fendall Hall which is owned and preserved as a museum by the State of Alabama. Fendall Hall is listed in the National Register of Historic Places. The keeper of the National Register has commented that the parlor and dining room are worthy of exhibition at the Smithsonian Institution. Built by Edward B. Young in 1854, and named for his wife, Ann Fendall Beall, this house merely suggested my story. Barbour Hall and the people who lived there are entirely fiction.

My characters were given added breath, however, when Purcell took me to Shorter Mansion, which is open to the public as a museum, and introduced me to historian and teacher, Mrs. C. E. Mundine. Elizabeth immediately became my friend and helper. She gave me the 1858 diary of Mrs. Elizabeth Rhodes which contained a detailed account of life in Eufaula. I acquired many books to research. Three of the most helpful were: J. A. B. Besson, *History of Eufaula* (Atlanta, 1875); Anne Kendrick Walker, *Backtracking in Barbour County* (Richmond, 1941); and Hoyt M. Warren, *Henry's Heritage: A History of Henry County Alabama* (Abbeville, Alabama, 1978).

Roseland Plantation and many of the mansions described in the story are beautifully preserved. Some of them are the residences of descendants of the people mentioned in *The River Between*. One of these gracious ladies, Mrs. James Ross (Emma) Foy, invited me into her home and shared love letters written in 1865 by Dr. H. M. Weedon and Mary Young. It was Miss Young who actually lived in Fendall Hall. This correspondence between young lovers separated by the river and the problems delaying their marriage provided a springboard for the correspondence between Lily and Harrison. I cannot thank Mrs. Foy enough.

I greatly appreciate the time Doug Purcell and Elizabeth Mundine gave not only in guiding my research but also in proofing the manuscript to be certain it is historically accurate.

For the visual trip down the Chattahoochee, I thank Marc Doyle of TV 5 WAGA in Atlanta for the use of their beautiful film, "River of Life."

I appreciate the research assistance given by the Lake Blackshear Regional Library, Jane Hendrix, Harriet Bates, and their staff.

Special color for this story was told to me by my friend, John Grover Cleveland Pace, who was born April 21, 1885, and at the time of this writing enjoys an active life with a sharp memory of events during his century of life.

I also thank the many other people who were helpful, especially my son, John Cook; my secretary; Mrs. Glenda Spradley; Mrs. Bill Story; Mrs. Ed Stephens, and Mrs. Lamar Bowen who went from the belvedere to the last page.

Eufaula is delightful to visit anytime; but it is especially lovely the first week in April during the Eufaula Pilgrimage (unless Easter intervenes), when the residents graciously open their historic homes to the public.

Jacquelyn Cook

ABOUT THE AUTHOR

JACQUELYN COOK brings a variety of interests to her writing, as evinced by the historical accuracy and spiritual quality of her books. She has been involved in various offices of her church since she was eighteen years old, and currently teaches Sunday school. Her extensive research—including the discovery of diaries and journals—of the steamboat era of the 1850s brings alive the gracious living of the times and people of Eufaula, Alabama.

Like her heroine in THE RIVER BETWEEN, Jacquelyn believes that "marriage is a total commitment based on the love of God, with each partner seeking the highest good of the other." To further prove her conviction, Jacquelyn happily relates that her own marriage exhibits her theme. She and her husband find great joy in their children and grandchildren. Jacquelyn is a prolific writer, contributing regularly to periodicals—from *Good Housekeeping* to *Western Horseman* . THE RIVER BETWEEN is the first of a trilogy of novels set in the romantic South.

Forever Classics are inspirational romances designed to bring you a joyful, heart-lifting reading experience. If you would like more information about joining our *Forever Classics* book series, please write to us:

Guideposts Customer Service
39 Seminary Hill Road
Carmel, NY 10512

Forever Classics are chosen by the same staff that prepares *Guideposts*, a monthly magazine filled with true stories of people's adventures in faith. *Guideposts* is not sold on the newsstand. It's available by subscription only. And subscribing is easy. Write to the address above and you can begin reading *Guideposts* soon. When you subscribe, each month you can count on receiving exciting new evidence of God's Presence, His Guidance and His limitless love for all of us.